Til You Come Back

to Me Again

Jewel Adams

Til You Come Back to Me Again

A Love Story

Jewel Adams

Jewel Adams

Library of Congress Control Number: 2014919004

Jewel of the West™

PUBLISHING

Til You Come Back to Me Again

Jewel Adams

"You are always new. The last of your kisses was ever the sweetest; the last smile the brightest; the last movement the gracefullest. When you pass'd my window home yesterday, I was fill'd with as much admiration as if I had then seen you for the first time...Even if you did not love me I could not help an entire devotion to you."

–John Keats

Jewel Adams

Orlando, Florida

I have been told that we all have defining moments throughout our lives. I can only recall two from my childhood. One was the car crash that killed my mother. That same crash left a long, horizontal scar just at my hairline. The second was the day my father and I left Italy and moved to the United States. For a fourteen-year-old, leaving my country was not a big deal. My family had traveled frequently, taking vacations for months at a time. Having inherited a fortune from his father, Papa provided us with a very comfortable lifestyle that we enjoyed. But Mama's death took away much of that joy. Papa said no one could ever take Mama's place in his heart and he never remarried.

The third defining moment came six months ago, when Papa told me he had pancreatic cancer. At twenty-two, I was about to lose the only person left in my life. It was a day of devastation, not unlike the day I lost Mama. After a great deal of crying and almost two hours of sparring with my Jeet Kune Do instructor, I'd sat down with my father and listened with a heavy heart as he gave me instructions and delivered his business and fortune into my hands.

When we first moved to the States, we'd traveled for a few months before finally settling in Orlando. Using his degree in hospitality and management, Papa opened *La Villa de Luca*, one of the very few five-star hotels in Orlando. At sixteen, I began working at the hotel, receiving training from my father in every aspect of the business. During my senior year of high school, I began taking an online course in hotel management, quickly earning my degree. With the years of training I received from Papa, I helped him run the hotel. And oh, how I loved working alongside him! His love of the business was my love. I aspired to be like him, a CEO and owner that the employees loved. Papa was such a smart man, a wise man. He'd also taught me about solid investing and had helped me to begin my own little nest egg.

Still, even with all the training and teaching, I felt unprepared to take on such responsibility. I felt unworthy of it all.

"You can do this, son," he had said, squeezing my shoulder with a hand that was already showing signs of frailty. "You not only have the knowledge you need, you have the heart."

Wiping the tears from my face before they could fall onto the folder of legal documents, I nodded and smiled sadly. "I'll try to make you proud, Papa."

Standing, my father pulled me up into his embrace. Even at fifty, he still matched my height of six-foot-two. "You've already made me proud, Angelo. You are a good man." He smiled, his eyes still holding the spark that never seemed to fade. "And with God's help, you will find a woman that will make you a better man." He rested his forehead against mine. "And though I will not be here, your mama and I will be watching you become that man."

How quickly the time has passed, Papa.

Drawing my thoughts forward, I stood by my father's grave long after everyone else had gone, taking a last moment to gaze down at the shiny black casket before the workers began their job of covering it with the waiting dirt. Closing my eyes, I held a carnation I had taken from the casket spray to my nose, inhaling deeply. White carnations were Papa's favorite because they were Mama's as well. For a while after she died, he'd purchased a fresh one each week and wore it on his jacket lapel. He said he felt like she was with him because the scent always reminded him of her. Papa wasn't a perfect man. He had many faults. But his love for my mother had been perfect–even when he sometimes did things that would make her shake her head in bewilderment–their love for each other had been perfect. When he'd made the decision to leave Italy, I had asked him, "Do you think Mama is unhappy about us leaving the home she loved so much?" To which he'd replied, "Not at all. She is very happy because she will be in the States with us too." I think that is why he'd purchased the four-bedroom Italian style home in Winter Park, even though there was just the two of us. Mama could never have more children after me, but she'd loved her space. I guess her sentiments had rubbed off on Papa.

But now I'm there alone, Papa. You should have thought of that back then.

Taking a deep breath, I tucked the carnation into my breast pocket, dried my face, and slipped my sunglasses on before turning and heading back to the waiting limo.

Jewel Adams

One

A Moment in the Elevator

One year later

The morning had been filled with one long meeting after another. The first had been with the management staff, during which we'd discussed the hotel and employees. Fortunately, there were no major problems and things were running smoothly as usual. The other had been with my accountants. Going over financial reports was oftentimes a little tedious, but knowing that books were balanced and profits and investments were still holding firm always brought a feeling of satisfaction that could not be measured. I walked away from each monthly meeting with the inner thought of, *I hope I'm making you proud, Papa*. I kept the same meeting schedule my father had always used–management meeting weekly and accountants meeting monthly–because it was familiar and it worked for everyone.

"Have a good afternoon, Mr. De Luca," Meg, the receptionist said with a smile as I exited the conference room.

"Thank you." Meg had been with us since my father opened the hotel. A few years younger than my father would be, she was married to one of the housekeeping managers. They were the parents of five and grandparents of two. "Have you given yourself another raise yet, Meg?"

"Of course," she joked. "That extra zero is gonna look good, as soon as the ink dries."

I chuckled. Her answer was always the same. "*Ciao*, Meg."

"*Ciao*."

Waiting for the elevator, I pulled out my phone to check for messages. There was a message from the man coming to tune my piano. He was scheduled to come at two, but had to cancel because of a family emergency. My father had bought the baby grand when I was sixteen and paid for me to take lessons. I still played every now and then, and I usually had it tuned three times a year.

There was a text from my good friend, Lee. We'd known each other since junior high and he was the first real friend I'd made when we moved to Florida. Lee, his wife, Kate, and I usually fished together twice a month. I took up the hobby right after Papa died and grew to love it. It was a time to relax and forget about the world, though Kate always spent a bit of it grilling me on my social life and begging me to let her set me up with one of her friends. I always said the same thing–I would think about it. Lee's text was a reminder for fishing on Saturday.

As I started to text a reply, the elevator doors opened.

And I saw her.

She was wearing one of the hotel housekeeping uniforms. Tall and leggy with platinum blond hair tied back in a ponytail, sea-green eyes, and a perfect face and form, the woman was absolutely lovely. She smiled and I smiled back, glancing at her name tag as I entered the elevator. She must have been a recent hire because I'd never seen her before. Her hands rested on the handle of one of the smaller cleaning carts, her nails neatly manicured.

"How are you, Suzanne?" I asked. Judging by the look on her face, my greeting had taken her by surprise. Her quick smile tuned into a wide grin that was completely adorable.

"I'm great, how are you?"

"I am well, thank you."

We stood silently looking at each other for a moment. "Are you enjoying working here?"

She gave me a peculiar look and it dawned on me that she had no idea who I was and probably found it a strange question.

"Yes. It's a great job, for now."

"Oh? Is this a temporary position for you?"

"Until I finish school."

"What are you . . ." I paused as the elevator door opened and Sylvia, one of the front desk clerks-and my good friend-entered. She had also been a good friend to Papa.

"How are you today, Angelo?"

"I'm good."

"So, you've met our Suzanne, have you?"

"Only just. She told me she is trying to finish school and I was about to ask her what she is majoring in."

Suzanne smiled again. "Fashion designing."

"You must be a creative person."

When she blushed, Sylvia said, "She comes up with amazing designs. You should have seen the outfit she had on when she came in to interview for the job. It was beautiful." To Suzanne she said, "Angelo here is the best owner ever. Apart from his father, I have never worked for a better person."

The young woman's eyes widened just as the doors opened to the lobby. We exited the elevator.

"You're the owner?" she softly gasped. "No wonder you asked . . . I do enjoy my job, sir."

I chuckled at her obvious embarrassment. "I know you do. And call me Angelo."

"It was good to meet you," she said, hurrying away with her cart before I could respond.

When she was no longer in sight, I walked over to the front desk and stood waiting for Sylvia to finish with an early guest check in. "Hey, I need to talk to you for a minute."

The older woman grinned and turned to the burly black man working the desk with her. "Carl, I'll be back in a sec."

"In trouble, huh?" He grinned. "Take it

easy on her, boss."

"Will do."

We went into the small office behind the desk. As soon as the door was closed, I grilled Sylvia about our newest housekeeper and she was only too happy to fill me in.

Suzanne Haynes was a year younger than me. Born and raised in Orlando, she was also an only child. Both her parents were teachers at an elementary school just a few blocks from the hotel, and had worked hard to give their daughter a good start in college, but she got the job at *La Villa de Luca* so she could begin to pay her own way–a trait that I found very admirable. Because she was so attractive, Suzanne immediately caught the attention of most of the male staff members and had kept it, but she never went out with anyone at the hotel. She was shy until you got to know her, and she loved to laugh.

"If you would like to know any more than that, then you'll have to find out yourself," Sylvia said with the signature smirk I had come to know so well through the years. Even when I was a teenager, I loved her smirk, and sometimes I used to wish she and Papa would become more than friends. But my father had still been in love with his wife.

"Maybe I will do that."

"Well, maybe you should. It's about time you got a social life."

"What do you mean? I do have a social life."

"You know what I mean. Fishing on Saturdays with your married friends isn't good enough. You need to get married and bless this world with children from your loins."

I snorted. "You just leave my loins out of this, Miss Busybody."

"I have to be, and I accept the title gladly. Someone's got to look out for you and insure that Gus has more posterity."

Smiling, I kissed her cheek.

"What's that for?"

"I appreciate you being such a good friend to my father, and to me."

Blinking tears back, she touched my cheek. "Gus was a good man. He would be proud of you."

"I hope so."

"But," she said, giving my face a light tap, "he will be bouncing off heavenly walls when you start getting busy."

"Sylvia! You naughty woman!"

"You know it."

Shaking my head, I chuckled and turned to leave, "*Ciao, bella.*"

"*Ciao*, Angelo."

* * *

When I got home, I walked back down the driveway to grab the mail. It was just junk, most of it addressed to my father. I sometimes wondered how we had wound up on so many mailing list when we'd hardly ever ordered anything through the mail. I quickly flipped through the catalog of sewing notions. I would definitely never have use for anything in it, and I didn't think quilting would ever be my thing. Placing my laptop bag on the kitchen counter, I tossed the catalog in the garbage and went up to my room.

Sitting on the edge of the bed to take off my shoes, I glanced around the room. When we'd moved in, my father had automatically given me the master suite and had chosen a slightly smaller room for himself. When I'd asked him why he didn't want the suite, he said, "Why would one man need a room this big?"

"Well, why would one young boy need a room this big?" I countered.

"Because one day that young boy will

become a man and there will come a time when he will not be alone anymore."

I had opened my mouth, then closed it. I had no response to that.

Now that I was living in the big house alone, I could see the true meaning in his words. It really was a big room for one person. The decor had evolved over the years. The old twin bed was replaced by a high, king-size, dark wood four-poster one. In the corner surrounded by floor to ceiling windows was a sitting area with a small sofa and a wicker coffee table topped with a few travel magazines and brochures. To the right of the double French doors was a high, black lacquered bistro table with two matching bar chairs. A gas fireplace with a beige marble mantle stretched across a corner, and above it hung a large flat-screen television with an audiovisual system built into the wall to the right of the fireplace. Plush light gray carpet covered the floor, and various prints of Italian landscapes and scenery hung on the walls. The walk-in closet was the size of an average bedroom, as well as the marble-tiled bathroom with its glass-enclosed, double waterfall shower and huge garden tub. When I was a kid, I couldn't truly appreciate these amenities, but I slowly learned to.

Breaking off my pondering, I undressed and laid my clothes on the bed and fished through the basket of freshly-laundered clothes for my swim trunks. I quickly put them on. Normally, I would have hung my suit up first thing, but I was anxious to get in a few laps and burn off some energy.

* * *

The adrenalin rush was stronger today and instead of doing the usual eight laps, I did twelve. Then I lay back and floated for a while, staring up through the glass ceiling at the clouds slowly moving in, creating a slight overcast. But it changed quickly and the sun's rays burst forth once more. The pool was completely enclosed in a spacious glass room so I could enjoy a swim regardless of the weather. I spent many a rainy day in the water. Sometimes, though, I would simply lie out on one of the chaises and watch the rain come down. Hailstorms were even more interesting to watch than the rain. It was an amazing experience watching ice–sometimes the size of golf balls–rain down on the ceiling. If I closed my eyes I could imagine hundreds of large birds pecking at the glass. I was grateful it was built so thick and sturdy.

I finally got out and grabbed a towel from the stack on the shelf and dried off, my thoughts drifting to Suzanne. I really wanted to get to know her, which would call for a little boldness on my part, a trait that until now I had only applied to business.

Two

Asking Out the Housekeeper

The following day I called Sylvia and asked her to check to see if Suzanne was scheduled to work. She was there. I quickly showered and dressed, choosing to wear jeans and a casual oxford instead of a suit. I didn't want to be intimidating in any way. I knew being the boss was intimidating period, but I was not going as the boss. I was just me.

Raking my fingers through my hair, I studied my reflection for a moment. People always said I was a younger version of my father. From the thick black wavy hair, blue eyes and small cleft in my chin to the way I walked and talked. We were close in build, but martial arts, running, and swimming layered me with lean muscle. However, before he got sick, my father had stayed in great shape.

Though I had been in the United States for over nine years, I'd purposely clung to my accent, and even though Papa was gone, I spoke to him in Italian each day. Doing this kept a part of him with me. I had even gone back to Italy for a two-week vacation after Papa died. Yes, I lived in America, but inside I would always be Italian.

Satisfied with my appearance–and hoping Suzanne would be too–I grabbed my keys and left.

* * *

"Thanks, Todd."

"You're welcome, Mr. De Luca," the valet said as I handed him my keys before casually walking through the sliding glass doors into the lobby, trying hard not to look anxious or anything. Heading to the front desk, Sylvia grinned when she saw me.

"Top floor," she whispered. I squeezed her hand, and as I headed to the elevator, she mouthed, "Good luck." I winked as the doors closed.

I got off on the tenth floor as another housekeeper got on. She looked at me curiously, yet there was a slight smile on her face.

"Good morning, Mr. De Luca."

"Good morning, Cindy. Could you tell me where to find Suzanne?"

"I think she just started on 1085."

"Thank you."

I headed down the left corridor, my eyes skimming over the green paisley print on the beige carpet. The walls were sea green with beige molding. A small black gondola was painted by each door, framing the gold plaques bearing the room numbers. When Papa built La Villa De Luca, he had been determined to bring the guests a taste of Italy. The building itself was built like a high-rise villa with peach stucco, a tiled roof, and wood shutters on each window. Flower boxes lined the top floor windows. The two penthouse suites had large potted grapevines growing across one side of the balcony. Though the rooms were carpeted, each bathroom floor and shower was tiled in mosaic, and Italian artwork hung on the room walls. Luxurious down comforters covered the pillow-topped beds, and a bottle of sparkling grape juice, a pair of wine glasses and a small tray of assorted cheeses and crackers were placed on a larger tray and left on a table by the window just before check-in. Our guests were always pampered and given the best service possible.

Reaching 1085, I slipped around the cleaning cart into the room. Suzanne was bent over the freshly-made bed, smoothing creases from the comforter. Before I could say hello, she looked up, startled.

"Sorry, I didn't mean to sneak up on you."

Her lovely face broke into a wide smile, the corners of her green eyes crinkling. "That's okay." She tucked a stray lock of hair behind her ear. "How are you, Mr. De –"

"Angelo," I said, gently cutting her off. "Please call me Angelo."

"Okay . . . Angelo."

"That wasn't so hard, was it?" I teased and smiled as a blush crept into her cheeks. She was absolutely adorable. "I know you might think this is extremely forward of me, but would you like to go out sometime?"

Her eyes widened. "With you?"

"With me," I said with a chuckle.

Her smile turned demure. "I would love to."

"Great. What is your schedule like this

week?"

"I'm off Friday and Sunday."

"How about spending the day with me Friday? Unless you have things to do that day."

"No, it's fine. I usually find time here and there to get things done at home."

I smiled, warmed by the joy in her voice. "Pick you up at 10?"

"That sounds good." She took a notepad and pen from the cart and wrote down her address and phone number. She shyly handed it to me and smiled. I took it, allowing my fingers to linger on hers.

"I will see you Friday."

"See you Friday," she said back.

* * *

"So how did it go?" Sylvia asked.

"We are going out on Friday."

"Yes!"

"I'm happy you are pleased," I said, laughing at the twinkle in her eyes. "I never knew you were such an astute matchmaker, Sylvia."

"Been in the profession for years."

"Well, thank you for your help, Yenta."

She laughed. "My pleasure."

I said goodbye and went out front. As I

stood by the curb waiting for the valet to bring my car, I pondered on Friday and what we would do, then figured it didn't really matter. Just being with her would be enough for me.

Three

Getting to Know You

Suzanne lived in an old apartment complex in Winter Park. Despite the peeling paint on the shutters and the broken concrete in the parking lot, the complex was pretty decent looking compared to some others in that area. It had a swimming pool, as well as a small lake that gave it a peaceful look. A family of ducks floated lazily away from the shore and a grove of trees stood to one side. It was a pretty picture.

When Suzanne answered the door, I was captivated all over again. She was wearing pink denim capris and a white peasant blouse. Her golden hair was down and hung just past her shoulders in deep waves. The eye makeup was a little heavier, but the way she wore it made her green eyes stand out.

"You look great," I told her.

"Thanks, so do you."

I grinned. Jeans and ribbed t-shirts or oxfords were my standard dress. "Thank you."

"Would you like to come in for a minute?"

"Sure."

When I stepped through the door, the soft scent of sandalwood gently touched my senses. While she went to grab her purse, I took a quick minute to scan the room. There was an incense burning in a wooden holder on the entertainment center. The modest but comfortable-looking living room was furnished with an old floral couch and chair. A crocheted afghan was draped across the back. An ivory lace runner lay across the chipped wood coffee table. There were a few faded floral prints on the walls, and sitting on a glass shelf was a framed eight by ten photo of Suzanne and an attractive dark-skinned woman with short braids framing her face. Her face and arms were a little too thin, but that didn't detract from her looks. In the woman's arms was a small child, maybe three or four years old. The little girl had a lighter complexion and wide storm-gray eyes. Shiny black ringlets hung down to her shoulders. She was beautiful, and I could only imagine how much more beautiful she would be when she was older.

Suzanne approached. "That's my roommate, Lila, and her little girl, Ekaterina. We call her Katia."

"How long have you been roommates?"

"Since we graduated from high school. But we've been friends since junior high." She tenderly brushed a finger across the glass. "Lila met this Russian guy right after we moved in together. A week later he raped her and took off."

"That is terrible!" I grimaced, swallowing hard. The thought of any woman being attacked or abused in any way literally made me sick. "Did they ever catch him?"

"No, and the next month she found out she was pregnant with Katia. The whole ordeal messed her up a bit emotionally, but she loved her child from the moment she found out she was pregnant."

I studied the photo again. "I guess she was wise enough to understand that it was not Katia's fault. She sounds like a very strong woman. It must be hard for her being a single mother."

Suzanne was thoughtful for a moment, her

eyes slightly sad. "She's making it. She wanted to meet you, but she had to leave this morning and will be gone until Monday."

"Well, I look forward to meeting her when she gets back." I smiled, attempting to shake off the gloom. "Are you ready?"

"I am." She took the keys from her purse and locked the door.

* * *

Even though Suzanne was born and raised in Orlando, she had never been to SeaWorld, so I took her there and we had a fun-filled afternoon. We played our own game of twenty questions and learned much about each other.

We walked through the shark tunnel, my favorite exhibit since I was a teenager. "Favorite book and why?" I prompted her.

"*The Color Purple,* because of the strength and courage of the heroine. Despite all the abuse Celie went through, she proved that we can overcome anything. What about you?"

"*The Hiding Place* for the same reasons. Corrie Ten Boom was a righteous and brave woman and an amazingly-selfless person. Now, favorite food?"

"Italian." She giggled at my wide-eyes expression.

"What a coincidence, Italian is my favorite, too."

"Favorite movie?" she asked.

"Anything with Bruce Lee."

"The karate film star?"

"Yes. And actually, it not just karate, he was the master of Jeet Kune Do."

"What's that?"

"Well, it is a martial arts system that encompasses physical, scientific, mental, social, and spiritual knowledge. It's an eclectic system, completely different from the other forms of martial arts."

"What do you mean?"

"Really it is all about using minimal movements and extreme speed to gain maximum effects. It's basically a set of tools that you use for different situations. Bruce Lee said that the perfect style was no style and you can use something from everything. You use what works and throw everything else away. He didn't like formalistic fighting. It makes sense."

"Sounds like you are really into it."

"I have been practicing JKD since I was seventeen."

"Wow! I feel safe now."

I grinned. "I am glad." And I really was.

"What is your favorite movie?"

"Gone With the Wind."

"My mother loved that movie, too. Even though Scarlett drove her insane, she still felt sorry for her."

"Me, too. But I mainly watched it for Rhett Butler. Ahhh, I loved him, despite the rumors of halitosis."

I snorted. "I guess with his looks, most women overlooked that problem. And I would think getting paid thousands of dollars to kiss him onscreen was a major incentive."

"You're probably right," she said, laughing.

I loved Suzanne's laugh. She was so bubbly and full of life, and having her open up to me warmed my heart. So far, it had been the perfect day.

* * *

That evening we went out to dinner, and of course, Suzanne chose Italian.

After the hostess seated us, our server took our drink order. I ordered sparkling water, Suzanne, a glass of red wine. I was never a drinker. Alcohol had never interested me because I saw its effect on some people. But it didn't bother me that Suzanne indulged.

"Thank you again for today," she said. "It's been a lot of fun."

"You are very welcome. I don't think I have ever had a more enjoyable day."

She smiled. "I feel the same."

Suzanne excused herself to go to the restroom. I watched her walk away, the gentle swaying of her hips attracting the eyes of many as she passed. She'd had that effect on men all day.

Throughout the afternoon, I had found myself silently asking, *Is she the one, Papa?* Then I would chastise myself for allowing my thoughts to move ahead so quickly. One step at a time. This whole dating thing was fairly new to me. In high school, I'd only dated a few times, one of those times resulting in me crossing into the forbidden territory of sexual intimacy. I had been so distraught over committing an act that should have been saved for marriage that I refrained from dating after that. Sure, the girl had been beyond forward and had practically begged me to cross that line, but it had been my choice to give in, and sex was not a thing to be taken lightly.

My thoughts again drifted to the tearful conversation I shared with my father when I got home that night and confessed what I had done.

"This was no simple choice you made tonight, son."

"I know, Papa," I said, wiping my eyes, my heart heavy with sorrow. What I had done could not be undone. What I'd given away could never be taken back. "I am so sorry."

"I know, son." He was silent for a moment, then his wise eyes met mine. "Did you use protection?"

I nodded, embarrassed by this part of the discussion. "She is on birth control, and she also had protection in her purse." I shook my head, pondering that fact. "I guess that should have given me a clue. Looks like she was used to nights like this."

"It looks like it," he agreed.

"I'm sorry," I said again.

Papa pulled me from my chair into his comforting embrace. "It was a mistake," he whispered. "One that you will never make again."

I promised him that night that I would never weaken that way again, and I intended to keep that promise.

Suzanne came back at the same time the server arrived with our drinks. We ordered our food and talked while we waited for the salads and appetizer. We started the questions again while we ate.

"What is your favorite holiday?" I asked.

"Thanksgiving. Yours?"

"Christmas."

"Favorite color?" she asked.

"I have two, gray and green. I love gray wool sweaters and the color of spruce trees, which I guess goes back to Christmas. And yours?"

"Red. I love red."

"Favorite type of music?"

"Pop and hip hop. Yours?"

"Blues and jazz."

"You seem like a blues kind of guy?"

"Really?"

"Really."

When our meals arrived, I ordered another sparkling water and Suzanne had another glass of wine. We ate our food, declining dessert afterward. Suzanne declared she was full, though she'd hardly touched her meal. I figured she probably was not a big eater. I asked her if she would like anything else and she said she was fine. The server boxed up her leftover food, I paid the check and we left.

* * *

"I had an amazing time," she said as I

walked her to the door.

"So did I. Thank you for spending the day with me."

"Thanks for asking me." Her smile was shy again, her eyes luminous in the soft light of the street lamp.

I wanted to kiss her, but with it being our first date, I was afraid she might think me too forward. She solved my dilemma when she leaned in and lightly pressed her lips to mine. They were soft and tasted faintly of the wine she'd finished before leaving the restaurant. I drew her into my arms, deepening the kiss as warmth filled my insides. It felt so good to hold her.

Parting my lips from hers I asked, "When can I see you again?"

"My evenings are free for the rest of the summer."

"Tomorrow night, then?"

"Sounds good."

I kissed her again and reluctantly said goodnight.

Four

Falling

"I had a date last night," I said, casting my line into the water."

"Wait a minute," Kate said. "*You* . . . went on a date?" She pressed her hand to my forehead and I snorted. "You don't have a fever."

"We're talking a date, date? Like, with a woman and everything?" Lee said.

"Okay, you guys, I am not sick, and yes, I went on a real date. And . . . we are going out again tonight."

"With the same girl?" Kate squealed.

"Yes, with the same girl, and calm down, you're going to scare the fish."

"Who cares, this is awesome!"

Lee grinned. "I knew you had it in you, bro. She must be something."

"She is pretty amazing."

Kate pulled her chair closer. "Tell us all about her *and* your date, and leave nothing out."

"Good grief, can't a guy keep some things to himself?"

"No," Lee and Kate said together and I laughed.

"Her name is Suzanne and you will love her." I told them how we met and shared what I had learned about her.

Kate heaved a girlish sigh when I told them about our date. Lee said I had forever ruined things for him because now he would have to start romancing his wife again. She said it was about time they did something more than pizza and bowling. I laughed as they went back and forth for a minute before kissing and making up. They were a good-looking couple–Lee with his wheat-blonde hair and hazel eyes, and Kate with her dark brown locks and chocolate eyes. Other than my parents, I had never seen two people more in love.

"So, when do we get to meet her?" Kate asked.

"Well, that depends on how tonight's date goes."

Lee handed me some lemonade, clicking his cup against mine. "We'll keep our fingers crossed for ya."

* * *

The rest of the summer flew by in a whirlwind of fun and romance. Suzanne and I saw each other almost every other day, and my feelings for her quickly grew. Many of our dates were spent at my home, cooking dinner together, going for a swim or watching movies. Sometimes we would sit out by the lake and talk. Suzanne always insisted that we take a blanket, on which we would lay and kiss, though I always had to call forth a great deal of willpower to keep things from going further. I tried to limit our time by the lake.

A few times we even invited her roommate Lila and her little girl to spend time with us at my place, or I went to theirs. Lila was very nice and looked exactly like her photo, and she was indeed too thin.

Katia was absolutely beautiful and I completely adored her. She had just turned four, and when she looked at me with those big gray eyes, she could get me to do anything. I even babysat her a few times to give Lila and Suzanne some time out together. Each time I did, I could not resist taking her shopping, and I usually brought her home with a few new outfits and toys. Suzanne and Lila were always giggly when we arrived, a sign that they had really enjoyed their time.

I fell in love with Suzanne that summer, and I wanted to be with her always. One night in late August, we ordered dinner in at my place. It had been a week of pondering for me and I'd finally come to a decision. I quickly set the wheels in motion, preparing for this night.

Over dinner, I told Suzanne I loved her. She said she loved me too. Placing a ring box in front of her, I asked her to marry me and she gave me an ecstatic yes. She quickly moved from her chair to my lap and kissed me hungrily, and my response was equal to the passion she exuded. I had grown used to the slightly-sweet taste of wine on her lips. The flavor was a part of her, and because she always limited herself to just two glasses, I was okay with that.

* * *

The following day, I told my friends the news. Kate was slightly subdued, but she and Lee congratulated me and said they were happy for us. Kate said we would have beautiful babies and I agreed. I couldn't wait to start a family.

I received congratulations from Sylvia as well.

"So, this is it, I guess," she said.

"You guess?" I laughed. "Yes, this is it. I have met the woman I want to spend my life with and I have you to thank for it."

"All I did was step into the elevator with you two. It's all about timing."

"Well, time was definitely on my side that day."

"I am happy for you, Angelo. I hope that you will be happy." There was a tone of graveness in her voice. I always called it her 'mothering tone.' "Be happy, Angelo."

"I will be." I squeezed her hand. "You will be there, right? For the wedding, I mean."

She smiled. "I wouldn't miss it."

* * *

We were married during the week of Christmas. Suzanne said she had always dreamed of having a Christmas wedding. The ceremony was held in the church she'd attended growing up. Lance and Theresa Haynes–though not well off–spared no expense, wanting to give their daughter the perfect wedding. They were

41

two of the kindest people I had ever met and we got along great. It had been a pleasure getting to know them over the months, and it was easy to see how much they loved Suzanne.

Lila was Suzanne's maid of honor and Katia was the cutest flower girl anyone had ever seen. Suzanne's dress was sleek silk and lace that hugged her curves. The train was long, as was the veil. She looked wonderful. I wore a classic black tux.

We exchanged vows and rings and were pronounced husband and wife. The kiss we shared was tender, and I marveled that we were really married. I was a lucky man.

During the reception, we mingled a bit, deciding to forgo a receiving line. There were endless congratulations and well wishes. We ate, danced, and reveled in our happiness. Suzanne had three glasses of wine.

Afterward, we flew down to Key West for our honeymoon. It was a wonderful beginning to the rest of our lives.

Five

Waking to Reality

Six years later

Hearing the front door open and close, I turned over in the darkness and squinted at the clock. It was two in the morning.

At least she'd made it home. Some nights she didn't. I was used to it now.

Turning onto my back, I raked a hand back through my hair, listening for her distant footsteps on the tiled hallway floor. She would tell me I needed a haircut again. She said the same thing each time she came in late, letting her hands roam in a clumsy attempt to initiate intimacy after being out all night with 'friends.'

My hair brushed my collar now, the black waves permanently tousled. I liked my hair this way and had no desire to change it. As long as I looked groomed, I was fine with it. I did still have control over some things.

I continued to listen for her. Her progress was slow, as always. While I waited, I again let my mind drift back over the years of our marriage. The changes had been slow, but each one served to further widen the small tear in my heart that had begun on our wedding day with that third glass of wine.

For the first six months, things were wonderful between us–not perfect, but I was happy starting a new life with the woman I loved.

We had agreed before our marriage that Suzanne would quit her job and focus on her studies to finish her degree. She had been excited about being a homemaker and had spoken of her dreams and how we would spend our time together. However, whenever I brought up the subject of children, she would change it. Over time, her dreams changed and her ambitions lowered as the glasses of wine increased.

She and Lila started spending more evenings out; I babysat, of course, which was the only part I didn't mind. Then Lila began to have increased emotional issues and Suzanne was away even more. She said she needed to be there for Lila and that I should understand. I wasn't happy about us spending so much time apart, but I did try to be understanding and sympathetic. Lila had been through a lot and it was only natural that she would lean on my wife. The two had known each other for years and there was a lot of history between them.

Two years later, Lila's drinking and subsequent drug use were the cause of her losing her job, so Suzanne started lending her money for rent and groceries. It became a habit and I told Suzanne that though I cared about Lila, I would not continue to fuel her addiction. She accused me of being too harsh. I also told Suzanne the best way she could help Lila was by example, hoping that she would eventually stop drinking too. Sadly, Suzanne still did not realize that she had a problem.

I finally sat down with Lila one day and encouraged her to enroll in a substance abuse program. She was wasting away before my eyes and I worried about her one day going too far. After weeks of begging her to get help for Katia's sake, she said she would, but only if Suzanne and

I agreed to be Katia's legal guardians. She didn't want to worry about her being taken care of while she was away. We agreed, I had my attorney draw up the paperwork, and everything was signed, filed and approved. We were now the guardians of a six-year-old.

The day we went to pick up Katia and take Lila to the treatment center, we walked into the apartment to find Katia's arm badly burned from trying to boil water to cook some noodles for lunch. The crying little girl was sitting by her mother, who was lying on the floor unconscious, a puddle of vomit pooled around her head. Lila had overdosed. We called the paramedics, but nothing could be done. She was already dead.

Because Suzanne was a wreck and inconsolable, I called her parents. They came to take her home with them. I rode in the ambulance with Katia and held her in the emergency room while the doctor treated her burn. I could feel the shuddering whimpers roll through her little body as she burrowed against my chest and it brought tears to my own eyes. Both our worlds were turned upside down. She'd just lost her mother to a horrible death, I had lost a dear friend, and I felt like I was losing my wife too. At that moment, I didn't know what to do or what to think.

Suzanne's father had kindly followed the ambulance in my car before he and his wife took Suzanne to their place. When Katia's arm had been treated, I drove back to what was once her home to get some of her things. I did not want to take Katia inside, so I had her wait in the car. She was already traumatized enough and I didn't want to make it worse. Running inside, I quickly gathered what I could and put it all in a garbage sack since that was the only thing I could find that would fit everything. I had no desire to search Lila's room for anything more sufficient, wanting to avoid seeing the spot where her body had lain.

When we reached home, I grabbed the sack and carried Katia inside, moved to tears again as her little arms clung to my neck. I ended up rocking her to sleep that night.

After that, Suzanne's drinking worsened and I felt like a single parent most of the time. When she was home, she sat around with a wine glass in her hand for the most part. She'd cry over the loss of her friend and I would try to comfort her. Sometimes she would let me, sometimes I couldn't get near her. She would drink until she passed out.

I spent many nights in the family room,

holding Katia and rocking her until she cried herself to sleep and I could put her in bed. I never realized a heart could break into so many pieces, but mine had, and I had no idea how to put it back together.

I tried to remember when Suzanne's drinking had become so bad. How had I missed the signs? Then I realized the signs were there from the beginning, I had just refused to acknowledge them. How could I have been so blind?

One day Sylvia confessed to me that she had become a little concerned about Suzanne before the wedding when Suzanne and Lila stopped by the hotel one evening to check her work schedule. She could tell they had been drinking, but she thought I knew, so she never said anything, feeling that it wasn't her business. She said she was sorry and I told her she had nothing to apologize for.

I stopped allowing Suzanne to drive, which angered her at first, but she soon realized it was for the best. On the road, she was not just a danger to herself. With the help of Lance and Theresa, and hours of talking to Suzanne, we finally convinced her to enter a program to get the help she needed. I promised her that I would always be there for her and reiterated that she needed to do this not only for herself, but for her family. After all, she was a mother now.

Her progress was slow but steady, and when she finally made it to thirty days of sobriety, we all went out to celebrate. I began to feel close to my wife again, and that night we made love for the first time in months. With each day that passed, I watched her change. She began to concentrate on growing her fashion career, and she doted on Katia. We began to dream together again, and plan for Katia's future.

Six months later, a visit from two old high school friends–both of them male–changed everything.

The drinking started again, along with the late nights. Sometimes when she came home, there was a scent permeating around her that I remembered from high school. There were a few kids who smoked marijuana in their cars before coming to class. It was a strong smell, one that stayed in your memory once you got a whiff of it. That smell was now surrounding my wife regularly.

One day I finally confronted her about it, stunned when she turned on me and screamed that it was none of my business. "You don't own me!" she yelled. I couldn't believe we had come to this.

Many times, I planned things to do with Katia and tried to include Suzanne, but my pleas went unheard. Every once in a while, we would come home to find that she had not moved all day. She would be sitting in the same spot in a t-shirt and pajama bottoms, her surroundings littered with empty beer cans and a wine bottle or two. The room always stunk of alcohol and I'd have to open windows and spray the area down to get rid of the smell. Like Lila, Suzanne was wasting away before my very eyes and I had no clue how to help her.

One night as I sat by the lake cooling off from a sparring session, I whispered, "Why did you not tell me, Papa? I thought she was the one." I had not been prepared to hear my father's soft reply.

"You asked me, but why? Why did you not ask God, son?"

With that answer came a bitter truth. My pride and neglect to call upon God had caused me to make one of the biggest mistakes of my life. I prayed on a regular basis. I always had, but not about marrying Suzanne. Upon that realization, I immediately apologized to God and asked for forgiveness.

Then I thought about Katia. Having her in my life was not a mistake. She was the one bright spot in all of this.

But what now, God? I wondered, my thoughts drawn to the present as Suzanne opened the door. Light from the nightlight in the hallway spilled into the room.

As usual, she said nothing until she undressed and fell into bed. Rolling over to me, she ran her fingers through my hair clumsily. "Need a haircut, babe." Her words were more slurred than usual, her breath and body smelling like a distillery. When her hand wandered over my chest, I lightly pushed it away. Less than a moment later, she was asleep. Feeling numb, I got up and went down to the family room.

Grabbing the remote, I slowly flipped through the channels. Of the eighty channels, over half were airing infomercials. The rest had nothing on that interested me. Turning the television off, I put my feet up, lay back against the pillow and closed my eyes. I was tired and empty. And I didn't want to do this anymore. I had promised to stand by Suzanne, but that was back when the love was still there. Sadly, it faded long ago, and there was nothing I could do about it. Part of me would always care about her, but it could never be like it was before.

Six

Fragile Hearts

The following day I had meetings all morning, so I did not see Suzanne. I did leave a note on the counter letting her know that Katia was with me. When Katia came to live with us, I made the decision to teach her at home. Suzanne thought it was a great idea, but she never offered to help. She wouldn't even try, always using the excuse that she was too busy, which was not the case. It saddened me every time this happened. Suzanne was the only mother Katia had now, we were the ones she looked to for nurturing, and she needed all the attention we could give her.

Katia was ten now, and when I had

meetings, I usually took her with me. She would sit in my office and do her work while I met with management in the board room. I met with Tim and Andrew, my accountants, in my office, not wanting to be away from her for long.

Despite the tragic things that Katia had experienced, she was smart and very gifted. In addition to her school studies, she learned to play the piano so well, the student had become the teacher and I now learned from her. We also had a period when I gave her Jeet Kune Do instruction. I couldn't believe it when she came to me at eight years old and said, "Angelo, I want to learn karate from you." I had smiled and explained exactly what it was that I studied, thinking she would be put off because of all the training it encompassed, but she was even more eager to start.

Katia watched a concert on television one evening and came to me the next day wanting to learn the cello. I asked her if she was sure and she was adamant, so I bought a student cello, hired a teacher and she started lessons. She picked it up so quickly, the teacher was just as stunned as I was. She immediately moved on to the violin and the guitar, and I turned one of the extra bedrooms into a music room for her. Her instruments stood in every corner, and framed posters of great musicians hung on the walls.

A few months before Katia turned nine, she informed me that she wanted to start studying ballet, so I enrolled her in a class one afternoon a week. She advanced quickly and was now en pointe–an extraordinary feat. I had floor to ceiling mirrors and a barre installed in the game room that had been vacant since Papa bought the house. The room already had a hardwood floor, and she now used it to practice three times a week. I was completely amazed by her. She was a prodigy. Whatever she wanted to do, she did, and she did it brilliantly. There wasn't an idle bone in her body.

When I talked with Sylvia about Katia's gift of perfecting new talents, she helped me to understand that children dealt with experiences in different ways emotionally. Katia was a truly gifted child, and maybe her way of coping with the loss of her mother and the uprooting of her life was to learn new things, things she could focus on. Her growing abilities helped to keep her centered. And as far as stability, I was now the only permanent fixture in her life.

I watched her from where I sat at my desk with Tim and Andrew. She was working in her spelling book. Sensing my gaze, she looked up and gave me one of those adorable smiles that completely melted my heart. Then she lifted her hands and signed, "I love you, Angelo." Ignoring the amused grins of the two men, I signed back, "I love you, too, *tesora*." I did not know what the future held for Suzanne and me, but I did understand that Katia, my little treasure, needed me. If I did nothing else in this life, I would take care of her.

* * *

We wrapped up the meeting around two. I hadn't stopped for lunch and I was starving. Katia had eaten the snacks we'd packed for her and I worried about her being hungry as well. Sylvia had come up earlier and tried to coax her into going down to have something in the restaurant, but she'd wanted to wait until we could eat together. Sylvia knew Katia well enough by now not to push, so she just brought up a side of mozzarella sticks to hold her over for a while. Katia had thanked her, then brought the dish over to share with me.

After seeing the men out, I packed up my laptop and helped Katia pack up her things. "What do you say we call Suzanne and see if she wants to go out and eat with us?"

"Okay. Can I call her?"

"Sure."

I gave her my cell phone and watched with a smile as she called. No matter how much Suzanne neglected her, Katia was always thinking of her and she kept trying, determined to win her affections again. The problem was Katia shouldn't have had to try.

"No answer at home," she said. "Should I try her cell?"

"Yes. If she's out already, maybe we can meet her."

While Katia called, I looked over my appointment book and checked my schedule for the next week. Having covered everything that I wanted to today, I didn't have another management meeting until the following week. I considered asking Suzanne if we could do something fun with Katia, but I knew she would have an excuse. Still, there would be no harm in asking her. I sighed inwardly, suddenly exhausted.

"Who is this?" Katia asked, causing me to look up. It hurt to see the confused look on her face, because I understood without even having to ask. When she hung up, there were tears in her eyes. She handed me the phone. "A man answered and . . ."

"And what?" I said, pressing a hand to her cheek. "It's all right, sweetheart, you can tell me."

Tears rolled down her face. "Angelo, she was laughing and told him to . . . come back to bed." Her face crumbled and I held her as she buried it against my shoulder.

In that moment, I hated Suzanne. I hated her for hurting Katia, and for abandoning us both. I would have to forgive her, I knew, and not hold onto the bitterness, but at that moment, it was hard to think about anything except what Katia must be feeling. Her little heart was breaking, and my heart ached for her.

"It's all right, *tesorina*. Everything is going to be all right." I kissed her brow. "Let's go home. We'll stop and get something on the way."

Seven

The Meaning of Hurt

Suzanne called while we were eating. We had gotten pizza on the way home, though Katia hardly touched hers, still upset by the earlier call. "I am going to the den to talk a moment," I said, kissing her brow. "I'll be back." She nodded, the sadness in her eyes seeming to deepen by the minute.

When I reached the den, I closed the door. "Suzanne?"

"I'm sorry, Angelo." Her voice was slurred as usual. "I'm sorry. Secrets I've kept . . . so sorry."

"Where are you?" I asked, keeping my

voice even. She did not answer and I asked again, "Suzanne, where are you? I will come and get you."

"I'm sorry for hurting you, Angelo. So many . . . secrets. You deserve so much better than . . ."

For the first time in a long time, I was beginning to worry. "Suzanne, you need to come home, okay?"

"I miss Lila, Angelo. I miss . . . you are good for Katia, not me. I'm not a mother."

"Please tell me where you are and I will come and get you, okay? Tell me where you are, Suzanne." She didn't respond. "Please come home."

"I will. I love you, Angelo."

"Okay, just call a cab and come home, all right?" She didn't answer. "All right?"

"You didn't say you loved me."

The phone went dead and I immediately called her back. A man answered. "Hey, she's pretty messed up. I'm calling her a cab."

"Where is she? Who is this?"

"This ain't nobody, man. She'll be there."

"Who is –" The phone went dead again.

I took a deep breath and tried to stay calm. Needing support, I called Suzanne's parents and filled them in on the call. We stayed in contact regularly and they knew how things had been with Suzanne. Just like me, they were at the end of their rope and did not know how to help her.

"All we can do is pray," Lance said. His words sounded hollow.

"I know, and I will. But if she does not come home tonight, I am going to call the police. This time something is not right."

"Angelo," came Theresa's voice, "I need to talk to you. I need to tell you something Suzanne should have told you before you got married. It is only recently that Lance and I realized she hadn't. But maybe it will help you understand why Suzanne is the way she is."

"Okay," I said, bracing myself for whatever I was about to hear.

"Over a year before Suzanne met you, she was seeing someone. He fell in love with her and wanted them to marry, but Suzanne had other plans. She was setting her sights higher than a meager high school janitor." She paused, and I both dreaded and needed to hear what came next.

"Suzanne got pregnant, and as soon as she found out . . . she had an abortion."

Her words were a kick in the gut. "How

could . . . how could she?"

Theresa sighed. "I don't know, Angelo. I honestly don't. A baby wasn't part of her plans. When Suzanne finally admitted what she'd done, we were crushed. And the father of the baby was literally torn apart. By making that choice, she murdered our grandchild. She asked us to forgive her and we did, but the father never did. He finally left town and Suzanne never saw him again."

Secrets I've kept . . . So many secrets . . . The abortion. That was what she had meant.

"Suzanne knew what she had done was wrong," Theresa continued, "and she realized it was something she would have to live with for the rest of her life. As much as we loved our daughter, she was a selfish person and I knew we were partly to blame for indulging her too much. But then she began to change and we did whatever we could to help her.

"When she met you, she was genuinely taken with you. However, it soon became obvious to us that your feelings were far deeper than hers, but we really thought she would truly grow to love you the way you deserved to be loved. We thought marrying you would finally get her away from Lila. It seems their friendship was stronger than we realized. And instead of marriage and motherhood helping her to finally settle, she has become even more destructive.

"Thinking on it today, it finally dawned on us that she never got over what she did, and substance abuse was her way of trying to forget, only now, with the loss of Lila, she is far worse."

I didn't know what to say to any of it. I was numb. It seemed I did not know Suzanne at all. I never did. Searching my feelings, I realized I felt absolutely nothing, and for the moment, I latched onto that.

Theresa apologized for her daughter and asked me to forgive them for not telling me. I assured her it was not their fault and I held nothing against them. It had not been their place to tell me. I also promised that I would never mention it to Suzanne or anyone else.

After ending the call, I sat for a moment, absorbing it all, and one emotion finally brought some feeling back to my heart. Pity. We humans never stop to think about how our choices will affect others. We think our destructive actions will only hurt ourselves, but the fact is our emotional hurricanes leave others hurting in their wake. Why do we not think of this?

Like the choice I made as a teenager to

have sex before marriage. My momentary lack of regard for such a sacred act hurt my father deeply, and had I continued on that path, it would have emotionally damaged us both. Thinking on Suzanne's substance abuse, it had started with just one drink, and that drink was the product of another choice. It had only been a bandage on a wound that had never healed.

The next emotion waiting to rear its head in my heart was anger. But I knew I needed to pluck that seed before it could fully grow–at least for now. What came through loud and clear was Suzanne never wanted to have children with me. She wanted my lifestyle, but not my children.

Shaking my head at the thought, I went back to the kitchen. The counter was cleaned off, the leftover pizza stored in a container. Katia was no longer there. I went up to her room and found her sitting on the bed with her arms wrapped around a stuffed bear that I'd bought her the year before. The sight of the tears trailing down her cheeks made my heart ache. I sat down next to her and she immediately moved into my arms. Pressing a kiss into her soft hair, I closed my eyes and rested my head against the headboard. We were both tired, and the past year had taken a toll on us. After today's revelation, I really didn't know how much more I could take.

"She doesn't love us anymore," Katia murmured, her face buried in my shirt.

"Oh, *piccola,* she is just sick right now. Her drinking is a sickness and she needs help."

"Why won't she let us help her? We could."

"I know, sweetheart. I want to, but she needs more help than we can give her."

"We can pray."

"You are right. Let's do that right now. Would you like me to say it or would you like to?"

"I will."

We knelt beside Katia's bed. I waited while she took a moment to ponder what she wanted to say. When she finally began, her words were few.

"Please, God, help Suzanne to know we love her. Help her to not hurt anymore. In Jesus' name, amen." She looked up at me. "Was that okay?"

"That was perfect." I hugged her and left her to change into her pajamas. A few minutes later, I returned to tuck her in. Then I kissed her and sat with her for a little while until she drifted off.

* * *

Half an hour later, the doorbell rang, followed by banging on the door. I hurried down to answer it, opening the door to a frazzled taxi driver.

"I can't wake her up! They put her in and said she was just passed out, but she's not breathing!"

My heart dropping, I bolted out to the taxi and opened the back door. Suzanne way lying down on the seat. Her hair was a tangled mess, her close rumpled, mascara smeared. I pressed my fingers to her neck. There was no pulse and she was already growing cold.

I called the paramedics, but when they arrived, there was nothing they could do. Suzanne was gone.

Hearing Katia yelling my name, I turned and caught her up in my arms, turning her away just as the paramedics were covering Suzanne's body. I was sure that just the brief glimpse of the still form lying on the stretcher would probably be enough to traumatize Katia. She wrapped her arms around my neck and cried, and I could almost sense what she was feeling. It was happening again. It was her mother all over again. The thought increased my own emotion. It was like a bad dream that I couldn't seem to wake up from. And I wondered if either of us would ever be okay again.

* * *

Three days later, we stood beside Suzanne's grave, staring at the bronze, carnation-draped casket hovering over the waiting hole in the earth. We were alone now, everyone having left us with their condolences and sympathetic pats on the back. Suzanne's parents had been the last to say goodbye. They had hugged us both and emotionally promised that they would always be there when we needed them. Watching them walk away, Katia squeezed my hand and tearfully whispered, "I hope God will never take you away from me, Angelo."

"Oh, *piccola*," I said, kneeling down and hugging her to me, my heart breaking all over again at her words. "I'll be here."

This graveside service had been no different from the one we had for Katia's mother. Both women had been troubled and lost, at least that's what was whispered around us during the service. Sometimes people had absolutely no tact. However, their words didn't make me angry, only sad because of their truthfulness.

As I slipped my sunglasses on, tightened my hand around Katia's, and we walked back to the waiting limo, I realized that, in a different way, we were lost now too.

* * *

Suzanne's death was legally ruled as an overdose. The autopsy had shown a mixture of drugs in her system and there were needle marks on her arm. The results had also shown liver poisoning. Her cell phone had been missing, and the person that put her in the taxi was never found.

Eight

Healing

Six months later

"Angelo!"

I'm coming, piccola.

Katia was crying again, calling out my name. When I reached her room, I whispered, "I'm here, sweetheart. I'm here." I lay beside her and she immediately burrowed against me. I held her until she went back to sleep. It happened once or twice a week, but it was less than before. She was getting better, slowly. When I first started having the bad dreams, I asked her to tell me about them and it was always the same thing; she was afraid of losing me too. I promised her each time that I would never leave her. It may not have been the best thing, but it was the only thing that would calm her. Now that the dreams had slowed down, I was sure she was starting to feel more secure.

A few months later, the dreams stopped completely, and I thanked God every day for sending her peace. I also prayed often that Katia would have a normal, healthy life, and that she would continue to grow into the amazing young woman I knew she would become, find love and be happy. I was so grateful to have this sweet angel in my life, and I hoped that divine intervention would always guide me to do what was best for her.

There were days that I missed Suzanne, and the emotional ache that I thought had faded would return. When those moments hit, they were painful, and the same questions would circle through my mind. Had I done all I could? Had I loved her enough? Did I give her the best life I could? Was I a good enough husband to her? Then I would mentally punish myself again for not counseling with God before I married Suzanne.

Sometimes I became so weighed down by these questions that the grief felt consuming.

Then Katia would approach me with sad eyes, put her arms around me, kiss my cheek and say, "I love you, Angelo. You're the best person in the world." The fog would immediately lift and I would feel whole once more. Somehow, she always knew and was there, like the Lord was working through her to comfort me. Her presence always reminded me that I still had so much to be grateful for.

Katia always accompanied me on my fishing days with Lee and Kate, and they were a comfort to us both. Katia absolutely loved it. She possessed a patient nature, so she made the perfect fisher. She was not squeamish at all about baiting a hook, and she actually loved the feel of worms squirming in her hand, not bothered by dirt in the least. When Suzanne was alive, I could never get her to come. Like everything else I suggested, there was always an excuse, so I finally stopped asking.

Kate, who had been unable to have a child, had just found out she was pregnant. I was happy for them. For so long, it had saddened me to think of them never having the opportunity to be parents, because I knew they would be great ones.

On one of our fishing days during a

moment that Lee had Katia occupied, Kate softly told me of her reservations about Suzanne before we married. Like Sylvia, she'd kept quiet about seeing Suzanne and Lila entering a bar one night when she and Lee were out because she thought it was none of their business. She apologized and I assured her it was okay, that I was okay. Sadly, it seemed everyone managed to see the real Suzanne–everyone but me.

Suzanne's parents kept in touch, checking on me and Katia. They still worried about me and felt a lingering sense of guilt for the way things ended between us. I told them I appreciated everything they had done and that we would be fine. Theresa said they would always consider me family. I appreciated that as well. They were still in a great deal of pain over the loss of their only child, yet their hearts were filled with kindness. They were good people.

Katia and I spent a lot of time down by the lake. We would sit on the grassy bank and talk about a variety of things–movies, books, things I did when I was a boy. I told her about losing my mother in a car accident, and Katia always touched the scar just at my hairline. My hair now covered it so well, unless a person was really looking, you couldn't tell. I talked about moving from Italy and about losing my father to cancer. We talked about the hotel and I shared my experiences working with my father.

"Do you still miss him?" she asked one afternoon as she tossed bits of bread out to the ducks.

"Every day."

She was thoughtful a moment. "Do you think he would like me?"

"He would love you as much as I do."

She grinned. "How much do you love me?"

"Hmmm, let me think. Well, do you know how big the universe is?"

"Nobody does. It's endless, like it goes on forever."

"And that is how much I love you."

Her eyes lit up and she crawled into my lap. She was still so small for her age. "That's how much I love you too."

I kissed her nose and hugged her close, inhaling the soft scent of her shampoo. "Thank you, *passerotta*."

* * *

A few weeks before Katia turned eleven, she said she wanted to have a birthday party and invite the neighborhood kids. There were only about ten kids that were near or around Katia's age and she didn't know any of them well at all. All the trials she'd been through had not given her an opportunity to be the social butterfly I knew she could be.

"It's about time I got to know them," she said to me, her expression thoughtful. She had the most expressive eyes, and the gray had deepened over the years. Her eyes were almond shaped and framed by thick, dark lashes, the kind of lashes many women would pay a fortune for. Her light voice had also deepened slightly, the tone of it a little raspy, which made her sound older than she was. Her hair, which had grown so much that it reached the middle of her back, was pulled back in a loose ponytail. I remembered having to brush and style her hair when she was younger. Sylvia taught me how because I was at a complete loss of what to do with a little girl's hair, and Katia's was especially thick. When Katia turned eight I began teaching her, and just like everything else, she caught on quickly.

"So, you are ready for some socializing, huh?"

"Yeah. I've put it off for too long."

I chuckled. "Well, I don't know. I might

have to give this some thought. We can't have you turning into a socialite just yet. You will only be eleven."

Placing her hands on her hips, she gave me 'the look.' "Angelo De Luca! If you don't stop –"

"Okay!" I said, throwing my hands up. I loved it when she turned into 'Little Miss Assertive,' and I always tried not to laugh until she did, which usually did not take long. "I will be happy to fund your grand soiree."

"Thank you."

"I guess we should make a list of people to invite and go shopping. Do you know what kind of cake you would like?"

"Not really."

"All right, we will look around. When you decide on a theme we can work on the cake."

Katia quickly made her guest list. She added Sylvia because she had grown to love her so much. Sylvia was truly the only other adult she completely trusted.

When the list was finished, we went to the party supply store. Katia browsed around a bit and finally decided she wanted the party to be a luau.

"Are you sure?" I asked with a surprised

smile. "I kind of thought you would choose a Barbie theme or one of the popular boy bands you kids are so crazy over."

"No, I wanted to choose something fun that everyone will enjoy. Besides, I don't really like that kind of music anyway."

"I know," I said, giving her hair a gentle tug. "I was just teasing my classical, bluesy girl."

"You know it," she said and I laughed.

We bought an assortment of colorful of leis, tiki torches, tropical tableware, tropical garland, hanging paper lanterns, party bags, and favors for the guests. We also bought a tiki piñata and enough candy to fill it. We then went to the bakery and ordered a large, two-layer sheet cake, decorated with tropical flowers, hula dancers, and mini surfboards. As far as food, to keep with the theme, we decided on pulled pork sliders, deli chips and pineapple punch.

After our shopping, we went to Katia's favorite Chinese restaurant for dinner. She was animated as she talked about the party and planned the games. I loved listening to her and watching her eyes light up. Once upon a time, I worried and wondered if she would ever be okay again, and though she still had moments of sadness, she was better. Her happiness was the most important thing in the world to me, and I would give her the moon if I could. There was nothing I would not do for her.

Jewel Adams

Nine

Growing Up

The day of the party arrived, and though Katia said she was excited and looking forward to it, she was in a somber mood. Sylvia came earlier in the day and helped us decorate the back patio. I picked up the mini buns and pulled pork from the restaurant where we'd placed the order, and Sylvia helped us make the sandwiches. While Katia went to change, I made the punch.

Soon the guests started arriving, each bearing a gift for the birthday girl. Katia thanked each person for coming and said she was looking forward to getting to know everyone. She looked like a little lady in her peach sundress with her thick curly locks pulled up away from her face, cascading down her back. She had a yellow flower in her hair that matched the lei hanging around her neck.

I stood by, looking on like a proud papa as Katia entertained and mingled. They played some games, ate, and took turns whacking at the piñata. Jared, a boy that seemed to be taking a keen interest in Katia, finally broke it. The kids scrambled around, picking up candy. Then Katia opened her gifts. She received everything from clothing to jewelry to gift cards. Sylvia gave her an art set, which she loved, and I was sure she would soon have a masterpiece fit for a museum.

Katia had received so many nice things, I wondered if my gift would pale in comparison to the others. I nervously watched her open the box. Then she smiled and cried, "Oh, Angelo!" and all my doubts fled in the face of her joy. It was a simple gift, really, just a book about Bruce Lee, a book of show tunes sheet music, a little pair of diamond earrings along with a gift certificate for ear piercing, and a framed photo of us that Sylvia had taken the month before during one of my meetings. Katia was sitting next to me behind the desk, looking over some papers. We were laughing and joking about her taking over my job. It was a priceless picture. And as she threw her arms around my neck and kissed my cheek, whispering, "This was the best gift ever," I knew it meant just as much to her as it did to me. The photo represented stability, another sign that I would never abandon her.

They played another game, then moved the party to the pool, but Katia did not swim. She and another girl just talked and watched the others. Twice, I caught Jared winking at her before diving in. At my raised brow and wide grin, Katia gave me a saucy look in return. I chuckled and kissed her cheek before going to grab more sandwiches for her guests.

A little over an hour later, the kids were done swimming and I helped everyone locate their clothes among the piles lying by the pool and handed out towels for them to dry themselves. Everyone thanked Katia for inviting them and she thanked them all once more for the gifts.

After the party was over and everyone had gone, Sylvia stayed and helped me clean up.

"It was a wonderful party, Angelo."

"It was, but I could not have done it without you. Thanks for your help."

"I'm glad I could be here."

Since most of the food was eaten (who knew kids could eat so much?) there were only a few sandwiches left over. I put them in a storage bag and stuck it in the fridge with the half pitcher of leftover punch. Then we took a garbage bag and gathered the few cups and plates left on the patio tables, as well as the wrapping paper and piñata debris. Finally finished, I stuffed the bags in the garbage bin and went inside.

"You're doing an amazing job with her," Sylvia said as I walked her to her car.

"Thanks." I heaved a deep sigh. "I never imagined my life going the way it has. There have been trials that I never thought I would experience, but I have learned much."

"And if you could go back and change things, would you?"

"Truthfully, I don't know. There has been a lot of pain, but there is joy too. That joy is sitting upstairs in her room. I would never change that. I would not trade *her*."

Sylvia smiled and kissed my cheek. "You're a good man, Angelo De Luca. Your father would be proud." She got into her car and I waved as she drove away.

"I hope so," I murmured, going back into the house.

Since it was not even eight o'clock yet, I decided to go for a swim. I went upstairs to change, stopping by Katia's room to talk about the party a little. Her door was opened slightly and I stuck my head in, surprised to find her lying on the bed curled up. My surprised quickly turned to concern when I saw the tears running over the bridge of her nose.

"Katia, what is it, *tesorina*?"

"It hurts."

"What hurts, *piccola*?"

"My stomach."

I pressed the back of my hand to her forehead and cheek. "Do you feel sick?"

"A little."

"Maybe you ate a little too much."

"But I hardly ate anything. And Angelo . . . there was blood . . . when I went to the bathroom."

Little alarm bells went off in my head, but they faded just as quickly as I realized what was happening. This was something I had completely forgotten we would one day have to deal with. I caressed her cheek. "Do you think you can get up to change into your pajamas?"

"Yes, but . . ."

"Just lie here for a bit. I'll be right back, all

right?"

"Okay."

I kissed her brow, whispering. "Be right back, Katoosha."

* * *

As I flipped on the light in the emergency storage room and grabbed the feminine products that Suzanne had purchased off the top shelf, I pondered and prayed for help in explaining to Katia what was happening to her body and the changes she would go through. Even though I knew it happened to many girls at this time, I thought it would be another year or two before Katia experienced it.

On my way back to Katia's room, I stopped by the kitchen to grab a glass of water and a bottle of pain reliever from the cabinet.

Sitting on the side of her bed, I gave her the medicine. Then, as simply as I could, I explained menstruation, told her about a woman's reproductive system, and how her body was changing and preparing for womanhood. After asking some questions, she said she understood. I explained how to use the feminine products, thinking she would be embarrassed by having me discuss this with her, but she wasn't. She went to change and got into bed. She was still in pain, but it was starting to ease up a bit. She closed her eyes and I sat with her for a bit, gently brushing the hair back from her face, caressing her brow. As the room darkened, she finally drifted off.

"*Ti amo, mi* Katia," I whispered as I kissed her cheek and left her to sleep. *My girl is growing up.*

* * *

As Katia grew, Kate stepped in and took her on girl shopping trips, helping her pick out things she needed as her body changed–things she should have had a mother helping her with. I tried, but I still had a lot to learn when it came to raising a teen, especially a girl.

She sometimes had mood shifts, but not many. In that way, Katia was not like the average teenage girl at all. It was as if she'd learned to master her emotions along with everything else. The two times that she did have bad moments were awful and I hated it because she would not talk to me at all, and we had always been able to talk about anything. Both times she tearfully apologized to me the next day. Of course, I quickly forgave her, then we went out for ice-cream. I learned that nothing won over a girl's heart better than chocolate ice-cream, or chocolate, period.

She began to take over the cooking. Armed with an American-Italian cookbook, Katia became a very proficient cook and I gladly turned the kitchen over to her. To seal her new status, I bought her a couple of chef aprons–one red and one yellow, her two favorite colors–and a plaque to hang on the wall that said, **Katia's Kitchen**. Many times, we would even cook together, even making a few of the dishes on the hotel restaurant menu.

Katia had a few sleepovers at Sylvia's place. Since Sylvia never had children of her own, she loved spending time with Katia and always had fun things planned. Sometimes Kate joined them and they made it a regular slumber party. Katia always came back the next day still giddy from the time she shared with them. I could never express to Sylvia and Kate how much their help and support meant. Because of them, my girl was slowly learning how to be a lady.

* * *

Once a month, Katia and I volunteered in the soup kitchen at the homeless shelter. The people that came through the line loved seeing Katia dishing out food. Her sweet smile always brightened the day of everyone there. Of all the things that she could be doing, she chose to spend time there with me, serving others. She did hang out a little with her friends and was indeed a social butterfly, but she preferred doing things with me. Katia was a people magnet and could charm her way into the coldest heart, and charm she did.

Sometimes we made our way to the residential part of the shelter where we would visit with the children and read to them or play games. The families loved any attention their children could get, and we always came away wishing we could do more. We made donations and kept them all in our prayers.

Katia even held a bake sale in the yard to raise money and she put together fun care packages for the children. Because of her selfless heart and the goodness of her spirit, she blessed the lives of all she came in contact with simply by being Katia.

* * *

When Katia turned fifteen, she finished school, having taken the SAT and the ACT and passing both with perfect scores. This was a major feat and I was proud of her. She had come farther and accomplished more than I ever dreamed, and to reward her for doing so well, we took a trip to Italy and Greece. We had taken many trips through the years, but never out of the country.

It was an amazing experience being back in my homeland. We spent the first few days in Rome, seeing the sights and visiting with people I knew growing up. I took Katia by my old home. The people living in the villa were friendly and had kept the place up well. They allowed us to come inside so I could show Katia around. She said it wasn't hard picturing me as a small boy roaming the halls there.

We shared a few meals with two families I knew well, and Katia came to discover for herself how dinner time in Italian families is always a major event. Since all the grown children lived in the same area, they shared dinner with us. Thanks to my lessons through the years, Katia was fluent in Italian and could follow the conversations easily despite how rapidly we spoke.

We spent two days in Treviso, two days in Milan–the shopping capitol–a day in Verona, and our last two days in Venice, saving it for last. Though Katia was used to living by a lake, waking to the view of the Grand Canal was a totally new and unique experience for her. Just as in the other cities, we filled the days in Venice shopping and touring the old churches, including the most famous church, St. Mark's Basilica. Both evenings, we took a gondola ride down the canal, and watching Katia's eyes light up filled me with joy. Venice during the day was pretty cool, but at night it was amazing because the entire city was lit up like Christmas.

On our final night in Italy, we stood on the Rialto Bridge. It was late so it wasn't as crowded. I knew Katia wanted to savor every last moment, so we lingered. As we stood watching the gondoliers steering late night passengers beneath us, I sensed her awe. This trip was a dream come true for her, and I hoped she would feel the same about Greece.

"Thank you for bringing me, Angelo," she said.

I wrapped an arm around her shoulders and smiled. "You are very welcome. I'm so happy I could share the country of my birth with you." I sighed, hugging her close. "No matter how long I live in America, Italy will always be home."

She looked up at me, not missing the melancholy filling my expression.

"Do you miss living here?"

"Always. But coming back makes me not so homesick."

"Can we come back again sometime?" She grinned. "After all, we do have to make sure you don't get homesick."

I laughed. "Thank you for being so concerned for my welfare."

"I do my best."

Chuckling, I said, "*Si, tesora mia*. We will come back sometime."

Ten

Day in the Sun

When Katia turned sixteen, I planned a Caribbean cruise for her birthday. I had always wanted to go on a cruise and when I mentioned my idea to her, she was ecstatic. The cruise would be a first for both of us. We were so excited about it, we even took a Latin dance class–at Katia's insistence. As usual, she was the perfect student, and I wasn't half bad, myself.

A couple of days before we were scheduled to leave, Katia had a few girlfriends over to share some of her chocolate birthday cake. Even though she told them they didn't need to, they brought gifts anyway. She really appreciated their friendship. Kimberly, Alison and Denise were fellow ballet students and they sometimes came over to put in a little extra practice with Katia, especially when there was an upcoming recital. While Katia was now finished with school, her friends were entering their junior year, and though they were all the same age, Katia seemed so much more mature. When Katia passed her tests, I had asked her if she felt awkward around her friends since they would no longer have school in common. She said no, and if anything, they envied her for being done. Still, the girls knew nothing would ever change Katia, which is why they loved her so much.

Two days later, we flew to San Juan, Puerto Rico and boarded the ship there. Since we would not set sail until ten that night, we put our carry-on bags in our rooms (I had splurged and gotten us both suites right next to each other) and went back off the ship, then we walked across the street to a pharmacy and bought two cases of bottled water to take on the cruise. Since we planned to spend a couple of days in San Juan when we got back, we decided to forgo looking around and just went back to the ship.

After putting the water in our rooms, we walked around the ship for a bit, familiarizing ourselves with the layout before heading to the Lido deck to have dinner. There was a grill close to the pool with tables to dine on both sides, as well as a buffet restaurant inside just beyond the grill area. We decided to have a little of both. Grabbing a burger and fries from the grill and salad and dessert from the buffet, we took our food to one of the tables out on deck and ate while listening to a live band playing island music. I glanced over at Katia to find her grinning widely and I laughed. She was positively giddy.

"Are you having a good time, Katoosha?"

"Definitely! And we haven't even left the port."

I laughed again, watching her as she took everything in, a festive feeling surrounding us. "I wish we were not leaving so late. I wanted to watch the deportation. But I guess we will have plenty of other opportunities to do that."

"I know. And just think, tomorrow we will wake up in St. Thomas. I'm so excited!"

"Really? I can't tell at all." I grinned when she gave me her signature smirk.

We finished our meal and Katia grabbed my hand. "Let's go, Angelo. I want to go look in the shop windows."

"Already making plans for my money,

huh?" She flashed that innocent little smile of hers and I chuckled. "Oh, all right, let's go."

On our way through the pool area, we walked by two teenage boys who shot Katia big smiles and I shook my head, laughing. It had started already. Standing at only four-foot-four inches, Katia now had the body of a woman, perfectly toned by years of dance and martial arts. Coupled with her beautiful face and long, thick curly mane, she was a recipe for whiplash and teenage male heart palpitations, because she definitely turned heads wherever she went. I was sure that when she attended the activities for her age group on the ship, she would not want for company. She was a good judge of character and I always trusted her to do what was right, and she never let me down. Still, I would have to keep an eye out for the wolf pups on the ship. I chuckled inwardly. If she knew what I was thinking she would be appalled and I would get a verbal tongue lashing that I was sure would start with her sassy, "Angelo De Luca!"

The ship shops would not be open until we were out at sea, so we leisurely browsed the merchandise in the windows. I could see Katia making a mental note of the things she wanted, and I would gladly get them for her. Despite the prominent lifestyle she had been given, Katia was not the least bit spoiled, and she was the most giving youth I had ever known. Sylvia always credited me with parenting success, but I knew Katia came to this earth with an ingrained goodness that only increased as she got older.

Later that evening after our luggage was delivered and we had unpacked, we went to our assigned muster station for the safety drill. Since it would not be much longer before the ship departed, we decided to sit out on deck and wait. Then the foghorn sounded and we slowly sailed out.

* * *

Katia knocked bright and early the next morning. I had just showered and dressed and was running the electric razor over my face when I opened the door. "Good morning, *tesorina*. I will only be a moment."

"That's okay, I know I'm early." She sat on the couch and waited while I put my sandals on. "Angelo, your hair is still dripping wet." She grabbed a towel and gently dried it.

I shrugged, glancing at the wet spots on my shirt. My hair was thick and now hung past my collar. "Well, I was trying to hurry because I knew a certain young lady would be eager to go."

She grinned and kissed my cheek. "Thank you. Okay, let's go."

I chuckled at her impatience and grabbed my wallet and room key, slipping my camera and passport into her tote bag. "All right, let's go, Miss Adventure Seeker."

We went to the buffet and ate a quick breakfast before heading down to the lower level to disembark.

* * *

The view of St. Thomas from the ship was beautiful, but riding the open-air tour bus around the island was amazing.

I perused a brochure that I'd picked up at the small visitor information building. A part of the U.S. Virgin Islands, St. Thomas was conquered by the Danish in 1666 and they took complete control in 1672. They divided the land into plantations, and the primary economic activity was sugar cane production. The country became dependent on slave labor and the slave trade during that time. For a while, some of the largest slave auctions in the world were held in St. Thomas, and the Dutch influence was still apparent today.

We rode through the narrow mountain roads, snapping photos of the tropical plants and trees. As we entered an area with small homes and apartments, the citizens waved and we waved back. The island people were very hospitable, making the tourists feel welcome and at home.

The bus driver dropped us and a few others off in the historic district, agreeing to come back and pick us up in a while. We visited Fort Christian, the Historical Trust Museum, the Emancipation Gardens, and toured the St. Thomas Synagogue, taking plenty of pictures along the way.

Katia grinned, squeezing my hand as we approached the famous 99 Steps (the brochure said it was actually one-hundred-three steps.) At the top was another set of steps leading to Blackbeard's Castle. "Are you ready?" she asked, her eyes dancing and I laughed.

"Lead the way, *tesora*."

We began our climb. When we reached the top of the second set of steps, we stood at the Danish watchtower known as Blackbeard's Castle. Built in the 1600s, the view from the tower was perfect for spotting enemy ships entering the harbor. The tower was surrounded by a hotel, a pool, and a snack bar. Katia took pictures of the pirate statues as we toured the grounds, and then

I took photos of the view from the top of the tower. A tourist asked if we would like him to take our picture and we said yes.

We purchased some t-shirts in the castle gift shop, making sure to get a pink one for Sylvia since it was her favorite color.

"Was it worth it?" I asked Katia as we made our way back down the steps.

"It was." She wrapped her arm around mine. "Thanks."

"You're welcome."

We caught the tour bus back the port, stopping for a moment to listen to some live island music. I put a few dollars in the donation can on the ground in front of the group. They gave us a wave of thanks as we walked away. We stopped by a few shops for more souvenirs before going back to the ship.

* * *

We had dinner in the formal dining room, sharing a table with six other people. There were two couples, and a mother and daughter who were seated next to us. It felt a little strange sharing the table with total strangers, but we weren't strangers for long. Everyone introduced themselves and we got to know each other a little. The woman's name was Cara and she was a single mother. Her daughter Shaylee was Katia's age. Cara was an attractive woman of average height and build with short dark hair and pretty brown eyes. Shaylee was a younger version of her mother.

The girls chatted quite a bit, oblivious to the adults. Since the next day would be a sea day, the girls made plans to spend some time together at Club 02, a club room where teens fifteen to seventeen participated in fun activities or just hung out. I was happy to see my girl making friends.

After dinner, I took Katia to the shop area, but she decided to wait for the sales before she bought anything, to which I responded with a hug, proud of her for being frugal.

After stopping by the rooms for a bit, we went to watch a variety show. We ran into Cara and Shaylee and invited them to sit with us. Cara took a seat next to me and Shaylee sat by Katia. The girls chatted while Cara and I talked comfortably until the show started.

It was a magic show, the magician also being a comedian. I was excited because I knew how much Katia loved magic and comedy, and the combination was bound to be good. And he *was* good. The tricks he performed along with his comedic timing had the whole audience roaring with laughter. Wiping my eyes, I glanced at Katia. She was smiling, but not laughing.

She was *not* laughing.

"Are you okay?" I whispered, squeezing her hand. She quickly grinned, but it didn't look entirely natural.

"Yes, I'm good."

"Are you sure?"

She nodded, her smile widening. "I am, really."

I frequently glanced her way throughout the performance. She laughed in all the appropriate places, but the mirth that usually filled her beautiful gray eyes was missing. When she caught me looking at her, she wrapped her arm around mine and rested her head on my shoulder. I pressed a kiss to her brow and figured she was probably tired from the full day.

After the show, I thanked Cara and Shaylee for sitting with us and wished them a good night. Shaylee told Katia she would see her tomorrow. When we reached our rooms, I asked Katia again if she was okay. She said she was just tired, then she hugged me and kissed my cheek.

"Goodnight, Angelo. See you in the morning."

"Goodnight, *tesorina*." I squeezed her hand. "Are you–"

"I promise I'm fine. Promise me you won't worry."

I smiled, cupping her cheek. "But that's my job."

"And you're so good at it," she said with a smirk and I chuckled.

"All right," I said. "See you in the morning." I watched her close her door and went into my room.

As I lay in bed, I pondered Katia's mood, hoping it really was tiredness and that nothing else was wrong.

* * *

Katia

Katia stood in front of the balcony doors and watched the moon's light reflect off the ocean waves. The day had been perfect. How could she let one remark bring her down and spoil her evening? She shouldn't have even been down. But when Shaylee had leaned over during the show and said, "My mom thinks your dad is hot," something inside her shifted. She didn't like the idea of Cara being attracted to Angelo. Ever since Suzanne broke his heart, Katia had felt protective of Angelo. She didn't want him to ever be hurt again. But she also realized he deserved to be happy.

Still, Katia had always felt that Angelo was hers alone, and she was not ready to share him with anyone else. She didn't know if she ever would be.

What is wrong with me? She knew she needed to snap out of this and overcome her selfishness, and she would.

She would be better tomorrow.

Eleven

"Be Like Water"

With only a few hours of sleep behind me, I was awake before the sunrise. When I had finally gone to bed, I couldn't turn my thoughts off, concern for Katia being at the forefront of my mind. I had observed Katia's shift in emotions in the past, but it was a very rare thing. However, there was something different about last night. I told myself over and over that it had been nothing, but my mind had not been able to let it go. She and I were so close, I was always aware of her, even when I was not with her.

Shaking my head at my over protection, I knelt by the bed and said my morning prayers, then quickly showered, shaved and dressed, wanting to be ready when Katia knocked.

Opening the balcony door, I stood with my hands resting on the railing, gazing out over the vast blue waters to the horizon where the sun was making its appearance, and I suddenly felt smaller than ever before. If the eyes were the window to the soul, then the ocean was the window to eternity.

The sound of the waves was soothing and tranquil, the scent clean and crisp. Closing my eyes, I breathed in the sea air, marveling at what an amazing creation the earth was. For a brief moment, I felt a solitary oneness with the ocean, like the large ship we were traveling on was completely mine and I alone owned this small part of the world. The wind whipping through my hair felt good, freeing. As I watched the ship effortlessly open a path through the water, I found myself pondering Bruce Lee's enlightening philosophy using water to describe human possibilities.

He said we should be like water, adjusting to an object and becoming shapeless, becoming whatever the water is put into.

Bruce was a great teacher and I could understand what he meant somewhat. I often pondered his words, and what I got from that particular quote was that we place so many limits on ourselves in life and we are always trying to fit ourselves into the world's idea of our potential. We have to expand our horizons and take in the lessons learned, then use what we've learned to shape our lives, placing no limits on ourselves in any way. The many obstacles in life should be treated as stumbling blocks. We trip and fall, then we pull ourselves up and get back on the path, adjusting our course accordingly to reach the goal. It is all about adaptability.

I smiled. If ever there was an example of that very philosophy, it was Katia. She was beautiful and brave, and she lived that way every day. She was my hero.

Emerging from the deep thoughts, I went back inside just as a knock sounded at the door.

"Good morning," I said, drawing Katia into a hug.

"Good morning." She moved back and gifted me with the naturally charming smile I was used to. "Are you ready?"

"Just let me grab my key."

* * *

After breakfast and another jaunt around the ship, Katia and I put on our swimsuits and went up to the pool. There were so many people, we couldn't do any real swimming. After a few minutes of floating in one spot, we got out and went up to sit in the hot tub, which was vacant at the moment. We stayed in for fifteen minutes or so, then we lay on the beach chairs and dried in the sun.

Heading back to our rooms, we ran into Cara and Shaylee. Katia told Shaylee she would meet her at Club O2 after she changed. Since the girls were going to be hanging out for a while, Cara invited me to go up and play a game of ping pong. Katia encouraged me to go, saying I need to do something fun while she was out.

So, Cara and I played a few games before moving on to shuffleboard, which was something I had never played before. I really didn't like it much, and playing it made me feel like I should have a senior citizen badge on my shirt. When I mentioned this to Katia later on, she just laughed and said we would have to play together before the end of the cruise.

* * *

It was the first of two formal dress nights. I changed into a black suit with a deep blue dress shirt and a gray and blue silk paisley print tie. Surprised that I had finished dressing before

Katia, I knocked on her door. She quickly opened it and rushed back to the sofa to put on her shoes.

"I can't believe you beat me," she said in a playful huff.

"I can't either. But then again, women always need more time when it comes to playing dress up."

"You're right about that," she said, finally standing.

I whistled. "Wow, *bella*! You look incredible."

She blushed, looking down at herself. She was wearing a long-sleeve black gown. The top had a mandarin collar with silver woven through the material. The skirt was flared silk that fell just below her knees. The two-inch-heeled black sandals with rhinestone butterfly accents elevated her petite frame. Her hair was down, the shiny black ringlets framing her face and slender shoulders. Because her lashes were so long and thick, she never used mascara. She only wore eyeliner, a hint of eye shadow, and lip gloss.

"Maybe I should go and grab my can of mace to fend off the ravenous teenage wolves."

"Angelo!" She laughed. "You're crazy!"

"We shall see."

"Well, you always look great." She

brushed the hair back from my forehead and softly touched the scar. I used to wonder why she always did that. Then I figured it was her way of saying I still looked great even with the scar. I thought back on Suzanne and how she always casually pulled my hair down to conceal it, even when my hair was shorter. Maybe that was part of the reason I grew it out. But I was used to the length now.

Smiling up at me, Katia took my hand and we went to dinner.

That night, Cara took a seat next to me. The skin-tight, low-cut red dress she wore didn't leave much to the imagination. And her daughter's dress was almost identical. Shaking my head slightly, I glanced at my girl's modest gown, grateful for her standards. I noticed Katia looking over at Cara, her expression blank. She quickly smiled at me and started talking with Shaylee about how much fun their afternoon together had been. Shaylee joked with Katia about how much attention she'd attracted from the guys at the club, calling her stuck up for not giving them the time of day, to which Katia responded, "I wasn't being snobby, I just have standards, and taste." Then they both laughed.

Taking a large gulp of her wine, Cara

scooted even closer and joked with me about my shuffleboard skills, placing a hand on my arm every now and then, and on my leg once. It had been a long time since I'd socialized with a woman this way, but I still remembered what it was like having a woman come on to me. It wasn't that I was uncomfortable, but I was not interested in what she was offering. A vision of an old *Love Boat* episode flashed in my brain. I had no desire to be part of a cruise ship match-up. I never cared for that show, anyway. Leaning toward Katia slightly, I draped an arm across the back of her chair, pressing a hand against her hair affectionately. She gave me a loving smile and continued her bantering with Shaylee about the 'stalker boys' as she called them.

After dinner, we all went to the atrium to listen to a little live music until it was time for the comedy show. The early show was supposed to be family friendly and Katia and I were looking forward to it. I could see there would be no need to invite Cara and her daughter. They were inviting themselves.

There was a brother duo performing in the atrium, one on a guitar, the other on the keyboard, and their vocals were great. They sang a couple of classic pop songs. The music was soothing and filled the atrium. I glanced up, taking in the people standing around the railings looking down at the singers. Everyone was enjoying themselves.

In the middle of the set, one of the brothers said, "Hey, we would like to invite a daring soul to come up and help us out with this next song. It's an old classic, and one I'm sure most of us are familiar with. So, do we have any takers?"

There was murmuring among the crowd, but no one was moving toward the stage.

"Come on, I know there's someone with a great voice. Who wants to give it a try?"

I scanned the crowd again, wondering who would be daring enough to go up. Then Katia released my hand and moved toward the stage.

What?

I thought I heard Cara and Shaylee saying something to me, I didn't know. I was so surprised by Katia's actions, words escaped me for a moment.

"Yes!" the singer said. "I knew there was someone willing to help us out." He asked Katia her name and age and where she was from. "Are you ready for this, Katia?" When she smiled and nodded, he said, "Okay, guys, we're going to do an Ike and Tina Turner tune. Katia, you know *Proud Mary*, right?"

"Yes, I do."

"All right, we've got the words here just in case you need them."

"I'm good," she says.

"Okay, guys, looks like we've got a little pro here. Okay, Katia, we'll harmonize with ya, but this is all you, so strut your stuff, all right?"

"All right."

It was surreal seeing my girl standing on the stage holding a mike, looking at me with that cheeky little grin of hers. Her courage never ceased to amaze me and I didn't think I could be prouder than I was at that moment, until she began to sing. My mouth dropped open in astonishment as she smoothly sang the first verse. Her voice was like liquid silk. Then the music increased in tempo and she belted out the lyrics, the silk transitioning into a raspy, soul-filled dynamic that shook the entire hall. Then the men began to sing, their voices soaring with hers, blending in perfect harmony. All around me hands were clapping, bodies moving to the beat. I could not believe this was really my Katia moving the crowd that way. It was a brilliant performance.

When they finished, the cheers and applause were thunderous. Everyone was actually begging for an encore. The duo praised Katia, telling her they had never performed with someone from the audience that was so good. Their voices blended with the crowd's cry for an encore.

Katia, said something to them that we couldn't hear. They nodded and she took a seat behind the unoccupied piano. One of the singers moved a mike stand by her and adjusted the height until it was perfect. They searched their tablets and found the sheet music to accompany her. She needed no sheet music, which amazed me.

She performed the classical-pop ballad, *Broken Vow*. I was completely mesmerized as she became lost in the music, and her piano playing was brilliant. Of course, it would be with all the years she'd spent perfecting her talent. Each lyric was sung flawlessly, and the raw emotion in her voice wrapped around us all.

Katia finished the song and again the hall rocked with applause. Both the men hugged her and thanked her for singing with them. People patted her on the back, congratulating her on her way back to me. She grinned and I swept her up in a big hug.

I drew back a little and beamed down at her. "Well, you are just full of surprises, aren't you, Katoosha? When did this new skill develop?"

Drawing my head down, she whispered, "I took some online lessons to perfect my singing voice. I figured I would surprise you one day."

I chuckled. "Well, you definitely picked a fine time to do that." She laughed. "You were wonderful. I'm so proud of you."

"Thank you."

Cara and Shaylee told her how much they enjoyed her singing. She thanked them and we made our way back up to the lounge, hoping there were still good seats available for the comedy show. "Amazing," I kept murmuring as we walked. She just laughed, holding tightly to my hand.

Twelve

Observations

The rest of the cruise breezed by. We spent the next day on the island of Barbados at a beach called "The Boatyard." Fifteen dollars got us in and included a beach chair, umbrella, and a free cup of fruit juice. We started the morning going scuba diving with the sea turtles and videoed with my underwater camera. The rest of our time was spent swimming and relaxing on the beach under the umbrella. We brought books and read for a bit, then we fell asleep for a while, making me grateful for the umbrella. Without it, we would have gone back to the ship completely fried. When we woke, the beach was filling with fellow tourists from the ship and I was glad we had gotten there early.

Natives walked along the beach selling jewelry, and I bought a turtle bracelet for Katia, as well as a necklace for Kate. We decided that we would leave soon, but for a short while we people-watched.

Many of the native men looked like Bob Marley, most of them donning hair longer than the women. The citizens of Barbados spoke English, but at times it sounded like a completely different language. When I had asked the scuba diving guide about it earlier, he said it was island slang. I guess if a person stayed on the island for a while, they would eventually pick it up.

To my left, there was a lady a few chairs down from us sunning and reading, holding a cigarette between the fingers of her free hand. She was a bleached blonde. The lines and wrinkles marring her face and body looked like they were the result of too many years in the sun, and I was sure she was younger than she looked. I tried to see the cover of her book, but I couldn't. Catching me staring, she smiled widely and winked before getting up and walking toward the water. She looked sickly and thin, like she had partied hard for too many years.

As Katia and I got up to pack up our things, a man approached us, trying to sell us aloe vera gel that he had extracted and squeezed into a pint-size rum bottle. I politely told him we were not interested and he moved on to the next person, only to have a policeman escort him off the beach because he did not have a permit to sell there. On our way out, we spotted the man by the exit and Katia slipped him a five dollar bill, earning a big toothy grin from him.

Smiling, I shook my head and draped an arm around her as we walked to the taxi area. I said, "You just could not resist, could you?" To which she replied, "He was an enterprising man, which is better than doing nothing."

My girl grew wiser by the day.

* * *

In St. Kitts the following day, we took another bus tour. In St. Lucia and St. Martins, we did more sightseeing and shopping. It was a good thing we brought two large suitcases and packed light. It was the only way we would get everything home.

On the final night of the cruise, we decided to order room service for dinner and watch the movie, *Somewhere in Time* on my laptop in Katia's room. It had always been her favorite movie, but this was the first time I had ever watched it. I'd always thought Jane Seymour was beautiful, and any movie she starred in was okay by me. The story was about a playwright who sees a photograph of a beautiful woman hanging in the hotel where he is staying, and falls madly in love with her. Then through self-hypnosis, he travels back in time to be with her. Katia had always told me how romantic it was, and since she loved it so much, I bought the movie for her before we came on the cruise. She'd saved it to watch on the ship. And she was right, it *was* romantic–tragically romantic.

The full day finally caught up with Katia. She was so tired, she fell asleep with her head against my shoulder. I turned off the movie, tucked her into bed, kissed her brow, and whispered goodnight.

As soon as my head hit my own pillow, I was asleep.

* * *

The next morning, we left the ship and stood in line with our luggage, waiting to get through customs. Cara and her daughter were standing in another line and caught us just as we'd exited and were about to cross the street. We were going to leave our luggage at the hotel until we could check in. Unfortunately, they were staying at the same hotel. I glanced at Katia and she quickly smiled. Again, it was not a real smile, but I gave her a look that said I understood. We only had two days in San Juan and I was not about to let them intrude upon our time together.

After spending the morning with Cara and Shaylee tagging along with us everywhere–and Cara trying to attach herself to me at every opportunity–we checked in and were heading up to our suite when I finally told her that it had been fun getting to know her, but the rest of the time would be mine and Katia's. While the girls took a moment to say goodbye to each other, Cara pulled a piece of paper from her purse, scribbled down her contact info, and handed it to me.

"Call me sometime," she said before brushing her lips against my cheek.

I smiled and we parted ways. Watching them exit the elevator two floors beneath ours, I felt as if a large weight had been lifted. Katia's soft sigh of relief echoed my thoughts.

We put our things in our room, took an hour to rest up, then headed out to see the sights of historic San Juan.

That night before going to bed, Katia said,

"Angelo, when we get home, I would like to get a drum set."

Thirteen

Suffering from the Same Sickness

Three years later

"I had a great time tonight."

"I did too."

"We should get together again sometime."

"Sure, I'll call you."

She kissed my cheek and went into the house.

As I drove off, I realized I always gave the same response. *I'll call you.* But I never did.

Over the past few years, Katia had encouraged me to start dating, and I did date here and there, but my heart was never in it. I could say I hadn't the faintest idea why, but that wouldn't be entirely truthful, because somewhere deep down, I did.

Katia told me it was because of Suzanne, and she said she was not going to stand by and allow me to be broken. I told her she was one to talk. She was nineteen now, and I could count the number of times she had dated on one hand. She said maybe she was broken, too.

The truth was I had absolutely no desire to date, and I was totally content with spending my free time with Katia. I was used to it. It was comfortable.

I knew that when I got home, Katia would be waiting. She always was. Her eyes would light up when I walked through the door and she would immediately ask me how my date went. Our conversations always went the same way. She would ask, "How was your date?" I would answer, "It was all right." Next, she'd ask, "What did you do?" Then I would tell her. Usually it was dinner and a movie. (This was what I termed the "safe date.") Katia always smiled, but it was not her real smile. It was her masking smile. There was something behind that smile I had yet to glimpse, and oh, how I longed to discover it, to see what that curved mouth and those slightly-dimpled cheeks concealed.

Hurrying home, I did my best to stay within the speed limit. I didn't know why I was always so anxious to get home. Maybe it was because I knew Katia would be waiting for me, or because I just needed to see her to make the night complete.

But when I got home she wasn't waiting. The house felt empty.

"Katia," I called, moving through the house. "Katoosha?" I looked everywhere.

She was not home.

She wasn't there and I felt hurt, even a little angry, but I quickly put myself in check and sent up a silent plea to God for forgiveness for the small moment of bitterness. It was not Katia's job to wait up for me. She was nineteen, a grown woman with her own life. Why should she be there? Just to feed my ego?

Maybe she's out on a date.

Sighing, I sat on a stool at the kitchen counter. Maybe the reason I felt this way was because for so long, *I* was her life, just as she was mine, and I didn't want to lose that. I didn't want to lose *her*.

Oh, heaven help me. What is wrong with me?

Not wanting Katia to walk in and find me waiting like a prison warden, I went upstairs and changed into a t-shirt and some denim shorts. I thought about getting into bed, but it was only nine, and I couldn't go to bed until she was home, anyway. But I needed to do something. I needed to talk.

Grabbing my cell, I dialed Sylvia's number. She answered on the first ring.

"Hi, are you busy?"

"No, why?"

"I need to talk."

After a brief pause she said, "I'll be right over."

* * *

Sylvia and I sat out on the back patio. There was a full moon out, illuminating everything around us. I could feel her looking at me, waiting for me to say something.

"So, did you really want to talk or did you just want some silent company?"

Taking in her deadpan expression, I smiled. Sylvia was always one to say what needed to be said. She never beat around the bush about anything. So rather than carefully thinking over my words, I said exactly what was in my head. "I think there is something wrong with me."

"How do you mean?"

I didn't stumble over it, I plunged straight ahead. "All right, I went out on a date tonight, my sixth or seventh in the last three years. As usual, the woman was nice and I had an okay time. But that's just it. It's always an 'okay' time. I can never enjoy myself because I spend the entire date looking forward to it being over so I can get back home. I wouldn't even go out, but Katia is always encouraging me to, yet she rarely goes out herself. She has always been home waiting for me when I returned, but . . . tonight she wasn't . . . and I was a little angry, and hurt. I mean, what is wrong with me? How can I feel this way? Why do I feel so . . . well, possessive? She is not a little girl anymore. She has a life and I can't always be a part of it. And that's what hurts most of all. I don't understand it. I don't understand *me*."

Sylvia sat forward in her chair and laced her fingers together. Even in the dim light I could see the signs of arthritis in them.

"You're right. She's not a little girl anymore, and she does have a life."

"So why is it so hard for me to accept that? When I think about her leaving one day–and she *will* leave–to make her own life without me, I feel ill and I have to push it from my mind. Why? There has to be something wired wrong inside my head."

"There is nothing wrong with you, Angelo. Simply put, you're in love with her."

Startled by her words, I jumped up from my chair and began to pace, my brain automatically brandishing my weapon of heated denial. *How could she say something like that to me?* "You're crazy! I can't be! I'm an old man!"

Sylvia laughed. "Angelo, I hardly think thirty-eight is old. I guess you think I'm ancient then."

"You know what I mean!" I practically growled, ignoring her attempt to lighten the subject. I hated the frustration ringing in my voice, but I couldn't allow my thoughts to even go there. "I am an old man in her eyes. Even thinking something like that would be like a dirty joke. At least, others would see it that way."

"But you *are* in love with her."

"I'm too old! I raised her. I am like a parent to her."

"Angelo, the bond you and Katia share has always been far beyond a parent-child relationship."

"What?! What are you –"

"Calm down, I didn't mean it like that." She eyed me for a moment. "What I mean is you were her friend, her nurturer, her caretaker and protector. You were her teacher and guide through those tender years. She depended on you for the unconditional love you gave her, even when Suzanne was here. From the moment you found her in that apartment sitting with her mother's body, it has always been you. When things got bad between you and Suzanne, Katia was your reason for going on, and your very existence was because of her needing you. You became everything to each other, because *each other* was all you had. I've watched you with her for years and I knew when she grew up, things would change."

Sitting back down, I released the breath I'd been holding and pushed a hand through my hair, raking it back from my face. "It just feels . . . wrong somehow." *It's ludicrous . . . isn't it?*

"But you admit that you do love her."

"I can't love her, Sylvia. It wouldn't be good for her. *I* wouldn't be good for her. What would people think?"

"Since when have you ever worried about what other people think?"

"She should be with someone her own age."

"Is that what you really want?"

I rubbed a rough hand over my face. "I just want her to be happy."

"And you don't think you could make her happy?"

"I don't know!" At the moment, just thinking about Katia being with someone else was more than I could take. As much as I hated to admit it, I was actually glad that she never went out. It meant that she was still mine. Looking back on the few dates that she had been on in the past year, I clearly remembered the dull ache that had grown inside me each time she left. And the last time she went out, I could barely concentrate on anything, and had spent a good part of the evening pacing the floor. At the time, I didn't fully understand it.

Reading my thoughts on my face, Sylvia said, "It would kill you to see her with someone else because *you love her.*"

Realizing it was pointless to deny it any longer, a slow, sad smile curved my lips. "With everything that I am. All right, there, I said it. But I can't tell her. She is still so young and I cannot risk driving her away. I could never forgive myself if that happened. Besides, she could never feel that way about me. She is probably tired of me already. She isn't even here tonight and she has always waited up for me. It just isn't the same anymore." A sudden sadness spilled over me with that thought.

"No, it isn't the same. It can't be. You are both consenting adults now. You can choose whether you really want to be together or not."

"I told you she doesn't have those feelings for me. How could she?"

Sylvia turned in her chair, facing me fully, her expression indiscernible. "Katia didn't happen to mention that we had lunch today, did she?"

"No," I said, surprised. "She didn't."

"I didn't think so. You two are more alike than you know. You say she hardly ever dates either, huh? I want you to take a moment and think about that. She is a beautiful woman, and I'm sure she has no problem attracting men. But ask yourself this question: Why would a woman want to go out with other men when the one who holds her heart is already there?"

My heart began to pound as emotion lodged in my throat. "What do you mean?"

"What I am saying is you and Katia have been suffering from the same blinding illness. You love each other."

"But . . . how could . . ."

"For you, I think it's a more recent development, at least in the last year. For Katia, I believe it started when she was sixteen."

"What? That's crazy."

"Is it? Why?"

"Because sixteen is rather young. How could she have those kinds of feelings then?"

"Do you remember telling me about the cruise?"

"Of course, I remember. It was wonderful and would have been the perfect vacation if not for that woman . . ." I stopped speaking as my thoughts traveled back to Cara's unwanted attention. I remembered worrying about Katia because she wasn't herself part of the time, usually when Cara and her daughter were with us.

"*Mama mia!*" I muttered, smacking my palm against my forehead. "I had no idea," I whispered. "How did I not see it?"

"Because you were in parenting mode, and Katia has always been good at schooling her emotions."

"I was hurting her and didn't know it."

"She was hurting, yes, but not because of you. She felt jealous and possessive, and protective of you. She had some idea at the time that her feelings were changing, but I don't think she really understood how much."

Sylvia squeezed my hand. "She loves you, Angelo. With all her heart, she loves you. But she needs some time. You both need time to learn to be without each other for a while." She paused. "Now don't be upset with me, but I have a beachside condo up in Nags Head. I offered to let her stay there for a bit, just to give her some time. She said she would like to stay for a couple of months. She plans to leave this weekend."

Her words were a blow to my heart. Katia was leaving. We would be apart for two months. Two very long months. I understood her need for time away, but the thought of not being with her–especially now that I had acknowledged my true feelings for her–hurt like hell.

But I would wait for her. I would give her the time she needed and wait for her to come back to me.

"I don't understand how this is happening," I whispered.

"I think it is happening because it was supposed to."

"But –"

"Don't question it. Just leave it in the Lord's hands."

* * *

It was a little before midnight when Katia got home. I was still up. I couldn't have slept if I tried, not until she was home. I met her in the upstairs hallway. We stood looking at each other, neither of us seeming to know what to say. I knew what I wanted to say, but I was afraid. Then something subtle happened. Like the gradual lighting of a room, what I had been seeking for so long appeared. The blinders were off, the mutual masks stripped away, and what I had only glimpsed for years was lying naked before me, and I was amazed. I finally spoke first.

"I talked to Sylvia."

"Oh." She closed her eyes and turned away from me. She was trembling.

"I had called her earlier," I said, not wanting her to think Sylvia betrayed a confidence. "Because I . . . needed to talk."

Slowly, I moved closer and gently took her shoulders in my hands, turning her around. I lifted her chin, urging her to look at me. There were tears in her eyes. I pressed my lips to each closed lid, and then her cheeks, gently kissing them away. I felt her shudder, felt the warm puff of air escape her as she exhaled. When I spoke again my voice was rough with emotion.

"Katia, *dolcezza*, I understand why you must leave. Take all the time you need. But know that I will be here waiting for you."

I drew her into my arms and she melted against me. My heart was pounding like mad and I was sure she could feel it. Her hands moved up my back and she held me tighter.

Neither of spoke again. We simply stood there, locked in an emotional embrace. I never wanted to let her go. I could hold her close to me forever.

Jewel Adams

Fourteen

Learning to Breathe

On the day of Katia's departure, I was an emotional mess inside, and I decided that Sylvia was right. We really did need to learn how to be apart for a while.

The past few days were eye-opening as we shared our thoughts, feelings, fears, and hopes. I had been nervous about embracing this change between us, concerned about the vast age difference, and about what others would think. I didn't feel good enough for her; I didn't feel worthy. But Katia's bravery soothed my inner concerns about me being enough for her. With love and tenderness, she helped me to see that I was more than enough.

We talked, laughed, and were our usual selves, only nothing was the same. There was a new awareness of one another, lingering looks and longing gazes. Katia was so beautiful. She had always been beautiful, but now I could appreciate that beauty as a man in love. The adoring smiles that once charmed me now warmed and melted me, making me feel things in ways I never had before. Everything she did or said now affected me differently. I could only describe it as flipping on a light switch in a dimly-lit room, suddenly seeing clearly everything I had struggled to see before. We did the same things we always did together, but now each activity was done with the knowledge that an unexpected future was before us.

And today she was leaving.

Before we left for the airport, I slipped something into Katia's bag and told her not to open it until after she boarded the plane. By giving her that gift, I was opening my very soul. I needed her to understand exactly how much she meant to me. She needed to know that she would always be my world.

Saying goodbye to her at the security gate was the hardest thing I had ever done. I held her tightly to me, pressing my face into her hair to hide my tears. I was torn up inside and could barely breathe.

She drew back and tipped her head to look into my eyes, her hand gently caressing my hair. "I'll miss you, Angelo."

"And I'll miss you." I caressed her face, longing to kiss her, but that would have to wait until she was home again and away from prying eyes. "Come back to me, *amore*. Please."

"I will. I promise." She kissed the corner of my mouth, lingering a moment. Then she turned and got in line.

I stood watching her until she was past security and no longer in sight.

* * *

Katia

Katia kept her emotions in check until she boarded the plane and was settled in her seat. She was flying in first-class, and so far, no one was sitting next to her. She discreetly turned her face toward the window and let the tears come.

Katia loved Angelo De Luca more than words could possibly express. She couldn't really pinpoint when she knew for sure, but looking back, she recognized now that her feelings for him began to change even before the cruise, they just didn't start to materialize until then.

Wiping her face with the back of her hand, Katia remembered wondering if something was wrong with her. And even though she had tried to shake it off and go on pretending things were normal, she couldn't. For her, everything was changing. *She* was changing, though she didn't realize just what was happening to her at first.

Many times during the cruise, Katia had caught herself staring at Angelo when he wasn't looking. Whenever they stood on deck looking out over the ocean, she found herself watching the breeze tousle his dark hair, marveling at the vividness of his blue eyes and the way his tanned skin looked in the sun.

She had felt an unfamiliar warmth curl in her stomach on the morning they docked in St. Martins when he'd opened the door to let her in before he had even put his shirt on. The muscles of his arms and chest were lean and chiseled. Seeing him without a shirt wasn't unusual, and during the cruise, she had spent time swimming and on the beach with him shirtless. But that day she was viewing him in a completely different light. Angelo looked like an untouchable Italian god. He was so handsome–he always had been, but only then did she truly admit to herself that she was attracted to the man that raised her, the man who had cared for her for most of her life.

Each and every day after that trip, her feelings continued to grow until she couldn't deny it any longer. She deeply loved him. She may have been young, but her heart had known what it wanted. Over the years, that want had become a need, one that was so strong, she could barely conceal it.

Drawing her thoughts to the present, she reached into her tote bag for a pack of tissues and her eyes fell on the small wrapped box and envelope Angelo put there. She dried her eyes with a tissue, opened the envelope, and pulled out the small note card.

My Dearest Katia,

There are so many things I want to say to you. I hardly know where to start, but I will share with you the most important.

First and foremost is that I am in love with you, il mia tesora. *You truly are my treasure, my priceless treasure, and I love you with every breath I breathe. You have been a part of me for a very long time, and I long to make you a permanent part of me forever. But that is a question I will save until you are home again.*

Just know you are in my heart, amore, *and my*

arms will ache until you are in them again. It is your
rightful place. It always has been.

Yours always,

Angelo

Katia closed her eyes and pressed the card to her heart, wanting to brand his words there. She had spent countless hours and moments dreaming of him saying those very words to her, but those dreams paled when compared to reality. During the past week, Angelo's words were guarded, measured. Now he had said it. He loved her. After all this time of loving him silently, to have that love returned was everything. But she still needed time to adjust to this new change in their relationship. She just hoped she would be able to survive the separation.

Placing the card back in her bag, she pulled out the box and unwrapped it, pressing a hand over her heart when she saw the actual ring box. She opened it, her vision immediately blurring as her eyes beheld the most beautiful ring she had ever seen. It was a one carat oval canary diamond surrounded by smaller stones and set on a diamond studded platinum band. Taking it from the box, she placed it on her finger. It was perfect, and the perfect ring for her.

Angelo knew her well. By giving her the ring, he was making a pledge and a promise, as well as claiming her as his.

She was all right with that. Because he was all she had ever wanted.

Putting the box and the card back into her bag, Katia spotted the bottle of ibuprofen and fished it out, dumping a couple into her hand as the familiar pain that had come and gone over the last year grew more prominent. The back ache and stomach ache were usually manageable and she had never felt a need to worry.

But now she had a future with Angelo to look forward to. And that changed things.

Fifteen

Oh, the Unpredictability of Life

I passed the days and weeks by keeping myself as busy as possible. I attended my weekly meetings, never leaving the hotel without a pep talk from Sylvia. Her words were always exactly what I needed to keep going. I increased my JKD workouts to three times a week and swam extra laps in the evenings. On my fishing days with Lee and Kate, I talked with them about Katia and finally told them of our feelings for each other, unsure of how the news would be received.

Kate had immediately hugged me, and Lee slapped me on the back and said, "I knew it would finally happen between you two. I'm happy for you, brother." Lee and Kate never really liked Suzanne and having their support now with Katia meant the world to me.

Katia and I talked every night, sometimes for hours. There were long moments when we didn't even speak, we just let ourselves *be* together, even though there were miles between us.

* * *

Sitting on the floor of Katia's dance studio, I closed my eyes and soaked in her essence. She'd been gone for a month and a half. You would think I would be better at missing her, but that just wasn't possible. I felt close to her in the studio, but truthfully, she was everywhere. There was no part of the house that I could enter and not see her in my mind. I really missed hearing her practicing, whether it was the piano or the cello, or even rocking out on the drums. I missed hearing the music, because where there was music, there was my Katia. Occasionally, I sat at the piano and played when the silence of the house was overwhelming. Then the memories of our playing together would flood my thoughts and that lonely ache would fill me anew.

Stretching out my legs and crossing my ankles, I leaned back on my hands as memories of another life made their way to the surface, and I took a moment to ponder my marriage to Suzanne. I had loved her and was sure we were meant to be together, but once we were married, her true colors came through clearly, and though I had started feeling like I'd made the biggest mistake of my life by marrying her, I was determined to keep trying, hoping she would change. When Lila died and we got Katia, I again held to the hope that Suzanne would change. Then I finally realized that she had to want to change, and she hadn't want it enough. But going through all of it led me to Katia.

Yes, I loved Suzanne, but when I compared it to what I now felt for Katia, there was no comparison, because loving Katia made me truly feel alive in so many ways. We knew each other so well that I was certain there was nothing we could not overcome. There was nothing I couldn't do as long as she was by my side.

Sighing, I lay on the floor and closed my eyes, wishing I could talk to my father. Even after all these years I still missed him, and I couldn't help wondering what he would think of Katia. He would love her, I was sure. He could not help it.

"I know you would love her, Papa," I whispered.

I had not talked to him in a long while, so I was surprised to hear his voice whisper to my mind, *"I do love her, son."* The comforting affirmation brought tears to my eyes. Then he said, *"I'm proud of you,"* and I wept.

* * *

Katia called me the next afternoon. She was scheduled to come home in two weeks and I ached to see her.

"How are you today?" I asked her.

"I'm okay."

"You don't sound okay." And she didn't. "What's wrong, *dolcezza*?"

"I need to come home early. I'm flying in tonight. Can you meet me?"

"Of course, I can. But what is it?"

"I'll tell you when I come."

"You've got me worried, babe."

"I'm sorry, Angelo. It's not something I want to say over the phone. I really need to wait until I see you."

The tears I heard in her voice made me anxious. "All right." I wrote down her flight number and the time.

"Angelo?"

"Yes?"

"I love you."

"I love you too. I will see you tonight."

As I hung up the phone, numerous reasons for her early return raced through my mind. One possibility brought too much pain to even entertain the thought.

Has she changed her mind about me? About us?

* * *

I had managed to convince myself that I was just being paranoid about Katia not wanting to be with me, and if there was some other problem, we would face it together no matter what it was. But as I watched Katia walk through security, the worrying returned with a vengeance. When she saw me, she rushed through the crowd and flung herself into my embrace. I again felt her trembling as I held her close. She moved her arms from my waist to my neck. Rising on her tip-toes, she held me tighter. Whatever was wrong, it was not us, at least I hoped it wasn't.

"I need you, Angelo," she whispered. "I love you and I need you."

"I am here, angel. I love you too, and I'm here."

She finally drew back and quickly wiped her eyes. I took her hand and we went to get her luggage. She was wearing the ring and it was beautiful on her hand. As we walked to the car, I was suddenly nervous and edgy. Not knowing what was going on was getting to me, but I did my best to exercise patience. Other than declaring how much we missed each other, the ride was mostly silent.

When we got home, I took her luggage up to her room and she followed. We sat on the bed and I took her hands. "Please tell me, *tesorina*. What's wrong?"

Loosening one of her hands, she softly caressed my face. Then, instead of answering right away, she unzipped her suitcase and removed a large yellow envelope. It was a medical envelope that said **test results** and had her name printed on it. I immediately pressed a hand to my heart, totally unprepared for what she was about to tell me.

"I've been having irregular periods for a while."

I forced my voice to cooperate. "How long is a while?"

She hesitated. "For a year now."

My mind raced. So, we will not be able to have

children. If that is it, we will deal with it together. We can always adopt. "You could have told me, Katia. You can tell me anything."

"I know, and I would have, but I read that sometimes it's normal. Sometimes there has also been a little pain in my stomach and back. I read that could be normal too."

"And sometimes it isn't," I said gently. "Did the doctor say you can't have children?"

She looked down for a moment. When she raised her eyes to mine, tears filled them and quickly streamed down her cheeks. "No."

Jewel Adams

Sixteen

Bittersweet Merger

Three weeks later

She was beautiful in her white gown. The silk, lace and tulle were accented by winking crystals on embroidered roses and flowed over her petite figure. Her hair was piled high on her head, held in place with a crystal-beaded comb, and a few curly locks framed her face. She wore no veil, therefore, there was nothing obstructing my view of her beautiful features. She looked like a princess. She *was* a princess to me. My tuxedo consisted of black slacks and a white jacket with a red bow tie and vest. Katia picked it out and I was happy to let her. Truthfully, I couldn't care less what I wore, all I could think about was she was really going to be mine.

Of all the defining moments in my life, the one that would forever stand out as the third most prominent, was the moment Katia softly spoke four words.

Stage four ovarian cancer.

Those four words changed everything.

She had already been through the tests, and when she got home, she went through another round the next day. The doctor said it was rare for a woman her age to have ovarian cancer, and because it had been growing in her body for so long, it was out of control. The cancer had spread from her ovaries to her liver and lymph nodes in her breasts.

We digested the prognosis. Then we had a choice to make: Katia could have surgery and treatments, granting her an extra month at the most, or enjoy the quality of life she had while she could. My sweet, brave Katia made her choice, accepting the fact that either way, the cancer would end her life. So, she chose to live her life and enjoy all the time she had left with me. She would take supplements and continue to exercise for as long as she could, and when the pain worsened, she would manage it with medication. Neither she nor I could think past that.

That evening I told her I needed to be alone and she let me. I went for a drive out to Coco Beach. I parked in an area that was not as populated and got out. Taking off my shoes, I walked the beach for an hour, trying to calm the anger that was eating my insides. I kept asking why. Why would God take her from me when we had only just discovered our love?

I finally sat down on the beach and dried my face as I gazed out at the ocean and watched the waves roll inland to lap the shore before receding and repeating the process. After calming my thoughts, I apologized to God for my anger. I had no right to be angry. Because she was His before she was mine.

That night, we lay in my bed, holding one another and crying for the shortened life we would have together as man and wife. Katia couldn't stand the thought of leaving me alone and it literally cut me up inside to think of losing her. I had only just realized my true feelings for her and now I would have to face losing her. We cried for the children we'd secretly dreamed of, children that would never be ours. I never knew I could hurt so much.

It was during this bout of pain that I finally kissed her for the first time. The kiss was sweet and pure, as a first kiss should be. But soon, emotion, both raw and desperate, seeped into the kiss, and heat rolled through me as the scent and taste of her filled my senses. I reminded myself that this was all new to her, and in a sense, it was new for me as well. Because the passion that the feel of her mouth against mine invoked was a level I had never reached before. I had never even been close. Having her in my arms was heaven. Exercising every bit of self-control I could muster, I parted my mouth from hers and just held her against my heart. Then we fell asleep.

The following day, we dried our tears and drew courage to the surface, determined to face everything head-on and enjoy the time we had together, which meant marrying as soon as possible. With Sylvia and Kate's help, we pulled the wedding together quickly.

Now here I stood, beneath the vine-covered Italian gazebo in our back yard, watching my bride slowly move down the white satin walkway on Lee's arm. All one-hundred-fifty chairs were filled, leaving me in awe of the support we'd received. No one had judged us when we announced that we were getting married. They were simply there for us. The only negativity we had gotten was from a long-time neighbor who felt it was her solemn duty to tell me how wrong it was to marry Katia and how much I disgusted her for taking advantage of such a young woman that way. Needless to say, she was not at the wedding, which was fine by me.

Kimberly, Alison and Denise also flew back to attend. When Katia and I first called the three and told them of our plans, each was a little subdued. But because they knew us well and had been a part of Katia's life for so long, they soon warmed to the idea of us marrying and were excited and supportive. All three had agreed to be bridesmaids, and they looked lovely in their yellow gowns.

Sylvia, Kate and Lee looked wonderful in their wedding attire as well. (Sylvia and Kate were Katia's maids of honor.) They were the only people privy to Katia's condition, and all three had tears trailing down their faces before the reverend began to speak. I knew it was only a matter of time before our tears joined theirs.

When Katia reached me, I took her hand in mine, never moving my eyes from hers. As we gazed at one another, it was as if we could see into each other's soul. I read her heart as clearly as she read mine. We finally turned to Reverend Sandler and he began.

"We are gathered here today in the sight of God to join Angelo and Ekaterina together in holy matrimony. As I stand here watching them together, I feel their love radiating around us, and I know that no two people were more meant for each other."

He smiled at us, his eyes misty. Reverend David Sandler had been a friend of Papa's, and even though Papa and I never attended his church, he had always been good to us.

"Now, Angelo and Ekaterina have written their own vows."

The reverend gestured for me to go first. Facing Katia, I held her hand against my chest, wanting her to feel how my heart beat for her.

"Katia, there are no words to describe what you mean to me. No words are good enough. You have brought such joy and happiness into my life. I love you so much, my heart can't hold it all. You are the air I breathe. I promise to love, honor and cherish you, and always be faithful to you, through the good times and the bad. My love for you is unconditional,

Katia, and I promise you that my love will see you through clear skies and stormy days. No matter what comes . . . I will love you through it, forever and beyond." I swallowed hard, blinking tears onto my face. I wiped away the tears trailing down hers, feeling the love in her eyes branding every part of my face that her gaze fell upon.

The reverend prompted Katia and she began.

"Angelo, you have been everything to me for as long as I can remember. You have cared for me, sheltered me, and loved me. When I thought that I had no one, you were there . . ." She paused as a river of fresh tears came. "And I know you always will be. I love you with all that I am. I promise to love, honor and cherish you, and always be faithful to you, through the good times and the bad. My love for you is unconditional, Angelo, and I promise you that my love will see you through clear skies and stormy days. No matter what comes, I will love you through it, forever and beyond."

Wiping his eyes, Reverend Sandler continued.

"Angelo, do you accept Ekaterina as your lawfully-wedded wife?"

"I do," I answered, firmly.

"Ekaterina, do you accept Angelo as your lawfully-wedded husband?"

"I do," she replied with equal firmness.

We then exchanged rings. Mine was a wide platinum band and hers was a thinner one set with diamonds.

"By the power vested in me, I pronounce you, Angelo and Ekaterina, husband and wife."

Needing no prompting, I took Katia in my arms and whispered, "I love you." She whispered that she loved me too and we kissed, holding tightly to each other as I took in the second most prominent moment of my life.

* * *

We quickly moved over to the reception area where we stood in front of an iron, floral-draped arbor and were congratulated, hugged and wished well. Sylvia hugged us both for a long moment and said she couldn't be happier for her favorite couple in the world. Lee and Kate quickly followed.

The band was playing one of our favorite songs and I led Katia up to the large, square platform for a dance. There were several couples swaying around us, but we were in our own little world. Katia gazed around for a moment, taking in the beautiful decorations surrounding us before returning her eyes to mine.

"Happy?" I asked.

She smiled, the warmth of her gaze heating me to the core. "Extremely."

"So am I."

"Thank you, Angelo. This is the best wedding day I could have asked for. Everything is perfect."

"You are perfect," I said, kissing her. She closed her eyes, resting her brow against my chin and I held her closer. We danced through another song before heading to the bride and groom table to eat.

The food was catered by the hotel restaurant and was perfect as always. Because ours was a traditional Italian wedding dinner, there were twelve courses, starting with antipasto appetizers and ending with a beautiful Italian wedding cake, made to Katia's specifications. There were plenty of food choices to satisfy everyone. No alcohol was served because neither of us wanted it, but the sparkling cider flowed freely and the guests seemed content with that.

We were toasted throughout the meal, receiving various wishes for a happy marriage, long life, and many children. Katia and I simply smiled at one another, silently speaking words of love and encouragement through our shared gaze. Yes, we were sad to know that some of the wishes were not possible, but we wouldn't let it get us down. This was our day. Our hearts were wrapped in love and we were warmed by the knowledge that we would belong to each other forever.

Since Sylvia, Lee and Kate were taking care of the reception cleanup responsibilities (they informed us that they were taking all the leftovers as an incentive) we finally left our guests and went into the house to change for our trip. We were going to Mackinac Island for our honeymoon. Katia's favorite movie was still *Somewhere in Time*, and she was ecstatic about spending our honeymoon in the place it was filmed. It was only because there was a cancellation that we were able to get into the *Grand Hotel.* Most reservations were done well in advance for this time of year. And as luck would have it, the room I reserved was a suite.

Katia's things were now moved in with mine, but we changed in separate rooms, which only increased our anticipation of finally giving ourselves to one another. I put our luggage in the trunk, and an hour later we drove off amid cheers and farewells and headed to the airport.

Seventeen

Memorable Mackinac

We flew into Pellston City, Michigan and took a taxi to the lodge where we had reservations for the night. The hotel was just minutes away from Mackinac City where we would then take the ferry over to Mackinac Island. To say Katia was excited was an understatement, but her loosely-contained giddiness brought me joy. Our room at the lodge was nice and cozy with a jetted tub directly across from the king-size bed, which was probably perfect for people staying there for an extended period.

Kissing my lips lightly, Katia went into the

bathroom with her overnight bag, closing the door behind her, and I took a deep breath and slowly undressed. Turning the bed covers back, I sat down and pondered this night. I would be her first and only, and she would be my last. I wanted to make it perfect for her, but it had been a long time since I was intimate with a woman and I was nervous. Waiting for my new bride, I felt like a teenager inside, but mentally, I had been seasoned by the years, and my mature emotions would hopefully serve me well.

Katia exited the bathroom, wearing a gown she'd purchased for tonight. She looked so lovely as she approached me, her gaze a mixture of innocence and sensuality in the lamp light. My hands were shaking as I drew her to me, but as soon as she wrapped her arms around me and pressed her soft body against mine, heat slowly flowed through my insides and the nervousness faded. The passion of our kiss increased, the taste of one another stoking the fire burning between us, each touch creating a mutual hunger and thirst that were only assuaged when we finally became one.

* * *

"I never knew it would be like that," Katia said, resting her head against my chest, looking up at me with a loving smile. "I've dreamed about it almost every day since putting your engagement ring on my finger, but . . . I never realized."

I caressed her face and kissed her, whispering against her lips, "It was never like this for me before."

She drew back a little, looking into my eyes. "Never?"

I shook my head, smiling at the wonder in her gaze. "Never."

Her lips curved in a trembling smile. "I'm so grateful to have experienced it, with you."

Her soft words pierced my heart, because I understood. The day would soon come when this part of our marriage would no longer be possible. But my love for her was so great and so deep, I could deal with the absence of sexual intimacy. I knew there would be times that I'd miss it, but I could handle it. Just being with her would be enough. I rubbed her back, caressing. "I am grateful as well. We must savor the experience while we can." Smiling, I kissed her again, whispering, "I plan to take advantage of every opportunity to make love to you."

She grinned adorably. "You took the words right out of my mouth, Mr. De Luca. So how about you take advantage of another opportunity now?"

"Mrs. De Luca," I murmured, rising over her, "you don't have to ask me twice."

* * *

The next morning, we had breakfast and checked out, anxious to be on our way. We took a taxi to the dock and boarded the ferry with our luggage.

Settling in our seats, we took a few selfie shots with my camera. I kept my arm around her and relished the wind on my face as we sailed to Mackinac Island. Katia excitedly tapped my shoulder and pointed to the Round Island Lighthouse, which was used for a scene in the movie.

The *Grand Hotel* soon stood before us in the distance like a beacon. Photos and movie shots were one thing, but actually seeing the grand building was something else entirely. Well over a century old, the hotel was a historical treasure. It was stunning.

When we reached the island dock, we grabbed our luggage and took a horse-drawn taxi to the hotel. Since cars were not allowed on the island, horse-drawn taxis, carriages, and bikes were the only modes of transportation. In fact, when they were filming *Somewhere in Time*, they had to get special clearance to allow them to bring the car that Christopher Reeve's character drove, as well as others that were needed for the movie. However, many things were in walking distance.

It was a surreal experience riding up the main road to the hotel. Katia was so excited to see the famous *Grand Hotel* sign, she squealed and hug me tightly. I laughed, welcoming her embrace.

We entered the lobby and I chuckled at the sound of Katia's dreamy sigh. Most of the decor was authentic and I could see her picturing the lobby scene from the movie. She stood gazing around while I checked us in. Then we went up to our room, taking in everything along the way.

Katia released another romantic sigh when we walked into the suite, and so did I. It really was beautiful. Completely decorated in an eclectic mix of nineteenth century decor and a color scheme of pastels and floral patterns, it was a Victorian lover's dream room.

The bellboy placed our luggage in the room, and though gratuity was already included in the honeymoon package, I gave him an extra tip anyway. He thanked us and left.

The anniversary welcome package I had ordered for us was combined with the honeymoon basket and sat on the table. It consisted of a hotel anniversary portrait by Marlee Brown, two bottles of sparkling cider (I had the hotel wine switched out) two glasses, the 125th Anniversary Book, a Christmas ornament, fresh fruit, a fresh cut flower arrangement, cheese and crackers, and a box of Chocolates. Also included would be cordials when they came to turn down the bed. Some people would probably consider this a bit much, but I wanted to make everything as nice as I could for Katia.

My mouth curved into a smile of contentment as I watched my Katia walking around the room, running her hand over the black gold-trimmed desk, allowing her fingers to skim over the matching foot-board of the bed. She turned to me and smiled, a look of yearning in her eyes, and I knew the unpacking would wait. I opened my arms, meeting her gaze with a look of mutual desire, and she moved into my embrace.

* * *

It was a little after noon when we made it down for the Grand Luncheon Buffet. The picturesque formal dining room overlooked the world's longest front porch–660 feet–lined with American flags. We were seated by the window, giving us a beautiful view of the Straits of Mackinac. On the buffet was a variety of rich foods–salads, cheeses, slow-roasted meats, seafood, pasta and vegetables. There were twenty varieties of fresh-baked pastries and Katia was in heaven, moaning with each bite. Katia enjoyed good food as much as I did, and I couldn't help chuckling at the twinkle that rose in her eyes as she perused the deserts. I had brought my camera with me and was videoing these moments. I felt like I needed to take photos and record every moment I could with her. One day I would need the memories.

After lunch, we looked around inside the hotel for a bit, taking a moment to look at the displays of items and props from the movie, including the famous portrait of Elise that had Richard transfixed. I read that Christopher Reeve didn't even see the picture until the actual filming so when he did finally see it, it would be a legitimate reaction. Having watched the movie and seeing his expression of awe, I thought that was a pretty smart idea. We browsed another moment before heading out to see one of the top places on Katia's list: the "Is It You?" tree, where

Richard and Elise met for the first time.

We walked down the boardwalk past the pool house and through the trees. The tree was located along the water's edge.

"This is amazing!" she said, standing next to the tree, reverently touching it, running her fingers over the bark. She read the plaque affixed to a stone.

"IS IT YOU?"
AT THIS SITE ON JUNE 27, 1912
RICHARD COLLIER FOUND ELISE
McKENNA

We asked another tourist who had just arrived to take our picture, and we imitated Richard and Elise's first meeting. The look of love in Katia's eyes was priceless. We thanked the man and left him and his wife to enjoy the site.

"That was perfect!" Katia said, hugging my waist. I stopped for a moment and held her close, kissing her softly. "I'm glad." I kissed her again and sighed dramatically, making her laugh. "So where to next, *bella*?"

"What about taking a carriage into town for a bit? Could we?"

"Definitely."

* * *

Walking through town truly was like

stepping back in time. We stopped by Baxter's Coin Shop where movie souvenirs were sold and purchased a few. Then we went to the theater where Elise declared her love for Richard during a play she was starring in. There was even a little plaque on the chair Richard sat in. To use Katia's words, it was pretty amazing.

We stopped in the fudge shop and watched a fudge-making demonstration. I loved fudge as much as Katia, and I bought a slice for us to share. By this time, I noticed how tired she looked.

"We should probably head back. I think we've worn you out."

"Maybe we should," she agreed with a smile. "They're probably serving dinner now, though I don't know if I can eat much."

"It's all right. Maybe there will be light items on the menu."

When we got back, we took our purchases to our room and changed for dinner. Katia loved dressing up and had even purchased a few Victorian blouses online to wear. The one she wore tonight was ivory embroidered lace with long, slightly-puffed sleeves, a drawstring waist, and a high ruffled neck with a cameo. She paired it with a cream-colored slightly-flared skirt. She looked fabulous. I wore the beige Armani suit Katia picked out, wanting us to blend together. I had never worn a suit so light in my life, but I did for her, and I had to admit, I didn't look half bad.

In the restaurant, we looked over the menu. We both chose the baby spinach salad and the mushroom tart, hoping the portions would not be too much. It turned out to be just the right amount, though Katia was only able to eat half, but she said it was important to leave room for a few bites of the salted caramel cheesecake. I told her it was good to have priorities and she laughed.

After dinner, we stopped by The Terrace Room for a dance. We swayed to a ballad played by the hotel orchestra, then we sat at a corner table and listened for a while, watching a few couples swing dance. Katia met my eyes, grinning, and before I knew it, we were up swinging right along with them. Katia taught me many dances through the years, and at that moment, I was very grateful for the lessons.

By the time we made it back to our suite, Katia was exhausted. She was experiencing a little pain, but she was still smiling. I grabbed some ibuprofen for her and she quickly took them. It had been a fun day, but I worried about her overdoing it.

"Tomorrow, we will take it a little easier," I said as we got into bed. I looked into her eyes. She was still smiling, but pain creased her brow a little. I touched her face and gently drew her close, suddenly wanting to cry. Swallowing hard, I turned off the lamp. "I'm sorry, *amore*."

"Shhh," she whispered, burying her fingers in my hair and drawing my head down, meeting my lips with hers in the dark. "I'll be fine," she whispered. "Don't worry. Will you just kiss me?"

Swallowing my tears, I did as she asked.

Eighteen

The Story Is Starting to Hurt

We spent the next morning walking around the grounds, taking in the beautiful gardens. The lush trees were over a century old, and there were over one-hundred-fifty varieties of flowers. The grounds were covered by blooms in an array of colors and was the perfect setting for weddings. The lilies and roses were Katia's favorite.

We made our way around back to view the 500,000-gallon swimming pool. I read that in 1947, Esther Williams used it when they were there filming a movie. At the moment, there were only a few people in the massive pool, but by the end of the day I knew it would be full.

After lunch, we took a bike ride to see some of the sites around the island. Katia was experiencing a little pain, but she managed it with Tylenol and ibuprofen.

We stopped to see Fort Mackinac. It had been the sentinel of the Straits of Mackinac for over two-hundred years. The guides were dressed in period costumes and we got to see cannon and rifle firing demonstrations. There were fourteen original buildings, and all were filled with settings for the period. We toured the exhibits and watched some of the videos.

The next place we went was to the butterfly conservatory. It was an all glass conservatory with lush plants surrounded by hundreds of butterflies fluttering around in special greenhouses while soft music played in the background.

"This is so awesome!" Katia said, holding my hand as we sat and watched all the different colors and breeds of the fascinating little creatures.

"It is pretty amazing."

She sighed, taking in the glass sections surrounding us. "You know, I read a book about a woman who had a near-death experience, and she said that in heaven the colors are even more vivid and beautiful than they are here. I'll bet the butterflies there are brilliant looking."

I opened my mouth to speak, but my voice caught and I had to wait a moment.

"I am sure you are right, *amore*." I was unable to say more. She turned and smiled lovingly and I knew no other words were expected or needed. I kissed her hand, holding it against my heart as we took another moment to look before getting up to leave.

* * *

That evening after we had dinner, we went back up to our room and watched *Somewhere in Time*. Katia said that since we were there, it was only fitting. This time I had a video cable with me, so we hooked my computer up to the television and watched it.

But this time, as I viewed the movie while holding Katia close, it was far more emotional for me. When we came to the part where Richard was showing Elise all the features of his 'decade old' suit and pulled out the dated penny that drew him back to the future, taking him away from Elise, I literally felt my heart break. And by the end of the movie when Richard was lying in his hotel bed dying of a broken heart, tears burned my eyes. I quickly blinked them away, not wanting Katia to think I was turning into a blubbering idiot. Then I heard her sniff and felt her tears wetting my shirt. I said nothing, just tightened my embrace, wishing I could take her into myself and keep her with me always.

After a moment, she sat up and smiled. "Tomorrow we'll go and see the gazebo and stables, okay?"

Caressing her cheek, I smiled back and said, "Okay."

Nineteen

Life Imitating Art

On our last morning in Mackinac, the pain began to worsen. We had just awakened when Katia sat up as it hit her harder than normal. She released a low groan and took a few deep breaths.

I kissed her brow. "Sweetheart, the Tylenol and ibuprofen are not going to work anymore."

She looked at me sadly. "I know." I wiped her tears away, trying hard to keep my emotions at bay. "Will you get me my meds?"

Kissing her cheek, I went to the bathroom and grabbed the large zippered pouch she kept her medicine and supplements in, grateful we had gotten the prescriptions filled. She normally took a vitamin along with large doses of ginger, ginko, vitamin C, a few cups of oolong tea, and over-the-counter pain relievers when there was pain. Now, in place of the over-the-counter medicine, she would take morphine, a low dose antidepressant, and another medication to control the nausea. She had put it off for as long as she could. Now she would have no choice. The doctor had been amazed that she'd stayed healthy for as long as she had. He attributed it to regular exercise and a good diet. I just constantly thanked God that Katia and I realized our love for each other before it was too late.

Filling a glass with water, I poured the recommended dosages from each bottle into my hand, then added her regular amount of supplements and took it in to her. Dumping all the pills into her hand, she took them all at once. As I watched her, I briefly wondered how long it would be before she could no longer do that. I quickly pushed the thought away. She lay her head against my shoulder and I held her as close as I could without hurting her. The last thing I wanted to do was cause her additional pain.

I reached for the bakery box on the

nightstand and gave her the last sweet roll to eat since she was supposed to take the medicines with food.

She took a small bite, then another and chewed slowly. "I'm sorry, *amore*," she said, touching my face. "As soon as the meds kick in I'll shower and dress and we can go."

"You have nothing to be sorry for. We can do whatever you want. I just don't want you to overdo it, all right?"

"I won't, but I don't want to spend our final day stuck in the room. Even if we just go out for a little while, I'll be happy."

"Just promise me you will let me know when you need to come back."

"I promise."

At that moment, everything inside me ached just thinking of her suffering, and I wanted to curl up in a ball and cry. But I needed to be strong for her. She wanted to enjoy our final day in Mackinac and that was what we would do. When she drew back a little and looked up at me, I smiled and kissed her lips. She gave me a brave smile in return.

"I think I can go and shower now."

"Okay, and while you are showering I'll order up some breakfast. Hopefully it will be here by the time you're done."

"Okay." She stood and leaned down to kiss me. "*Ti amo*, Angelo," she whispered against my lips.

"I love you, too, *dolcezza*."

I quickly ordered our breakfast and pulled on yesterday's pair of jeans. Then I knelt and prayed, thanking God for Katia, and tearfully pleaded for many more months with her. I stayed on my knees until room service knocked.

When Katia came from the bathroom, I had everything ready and we sat down at the table to eat. She looked at me a long moment, not missing the fact that I'd been crying. I smiled and she smiled back, tears brimming her tired eyes. The medication was affecting her already and I worried about going out. She suggested that we go sit out on the porch for a while and people-watch. I grinned, glimpsing the small spark in her eyes. She was being so brave. My brave Katia.

* * *

We did sit out on the porch and people-watch for a while. The row of white rockers sat pristine in the morning sun. There were a few empty ones between us and a small group of guests. The view of the sea from where we sat was incredible. We held hands and silently enjoyed the soft sounds around us. Then Katia suggested that we get up before she fell asleep.

We browsed the gift shop once more. I purchase a *Grand Hotel* music box for Katia, loving the way her eyes lit up as she gazed at it. It was a replica of the one Elise owned in the movie, and when you opened the lid, it played the beautiful Rachmaninoff theme from the movie. Katia in turn bought me a replica of the pocket watch Elise gave to Richard. On the face was a picture of the two lead characters.

"Thank you for this," she said, kissing me and hugging the package containing the music box. "Thank you for an amazing honeymoon." She smiled, her eyes full of love. "I feel like Elise and you're my Richard."

Oh, love, if I could only go back in time to save you . . . "Thank you for the watch, and for marrying me." I pressed a hand to her cheek. "And I doubt Richard could love Elise any more than I love you." She wrapped an arm around my waist and I held her to me, wishing I could find the words to tell her exactly what she meant to me.

We went back to our room and Katia lay down to rest for a while. I curled my body around hers and napped with her. When we awakened later, we ordered dinner in and began to pack. By the time our meal arrived, Katia needed to take more pain medication. After we ate, we changed and got into bed, leaving the rest of the packing until the morning. I held her for a while and we talked.

Glancing down at her arm, I lightly ran my fingers across the scarred tissue from the burn she'd gotten as a child.

"I probably should have had something done to it," she said, raising her eyes to mine.

"I'm glad you didn't." Raising her arm to my lips, I kissed the scar. "It is a part of you and I wouldn't want you to change it."

She smiled. "I can still remember the day a little. I vaguely remember getting the burn, but I do clearly remember trying to wake my mother up. Then you were there . . . and you made everything better."

I tightened my embrace, allowing myself to fully remember that day. Suzanne and I had been arguing. Again. I still wanted children, she didn't. But I soon came to realize it was for the best.

Katia's eyes turned misty, and I knew she had guessed where my thoughts traveled. "I'm so sorry that I can't get you a child, Angelo –"

"Don't be sorry," I said, brushing my lips over her temple. "You are enough."

"But when I'm gone –"

"I will have my memories of you. And I will look forward to the day when we can be together again."

"We *will* be together again."

Swallowing against the lump in my throat, I softly said, "We will."

Jewel Adams

Twenty

The Vows

Katia slept through much of the plane ride home. During the trip, I pondered how I had dreamed of taking her back to Mackinac one day for the *Somewhere in Time* weekend. She would have loved it. But now that dream, like so many others, would not be possible. The thought saddened me so much, I fought back tears.

On our way to the house, I stopped by the hotel restaurant and ordered some of Katia's favorite soup and sandwiches to go. When we made it home, I encouraged her to go up and change into her gown while I brought everything inside. She came down and we ate the meal, then we unpacked and put things away. I set the music box on her bedside table so she could always see it when she awakened each morning.

Katia finally took her medication and lay back against the pillows, watching me put the last few things away. I opened the music box and she smiled, her expression melancholy as the Rhapsody gently played.

I sat down on the bed beside her. "Can I get you anything?" I asked, brushing the hair away from her face, tucking a lock behind her ear. Her eyes suddenly filled and tears spilled down her cheeks. "What is it?"

"I'm just so sorry to put you through this."

"Oh, angel, don't be sorry. I love you. You are my wife and this is my place." She began to sob and I crawled over next to her and took her in my arms, pressing my lips to her brow and rocking her slowly. "Don't cry, baby. Please don't feel sorry." My own tears fell into her hair. I drew back a little and looked into her eyes. "Do you remember our wedding vows? We promised each other, Katia. I promised you we would get through this together." Holding her close, I softly recited our vows.

"I promise to love, honor and cherish you, and always be faithful to you, through the good times and

the bad. My love for you is unconditional, Katia, and I promise you that my love will see you through clear skies and stormy days. No matter what comes, I will love you through it, forever and beyond."

"That will never change, *tesora*." Pressing her close still, I silently pondered our time in Mackinac. "If there is one thing I have learned from the story of Richard and Elise, it is that true love transcends all things. Regardless of the circumstances, there is always hope." My voice cracked. "And though I will lose you for a time, I have hope, and the faith that we will be together again. I *know* we will. It is that knowledge that will keep me going on."

Katia touched my cheek. "I love you," she whispered, raising her mouth to mine and I let the passion of her kiss roll through me, latching on to all she offered, her sweetness consuming me. These moments would forever be branded in my memory, each one logged and filed in the annals of my mind, to be cherished, savored and experienced again when the day finally came that she was no longer beside me.

* * *

I woke up just after five. It was Monday and there were meetings scheduled. For the first time in a long time, I wished I didn't have to go. The thought of being away from Katia was physically painful, and before going to sleep last night, I pondered conducting my meetings from home via the internet. My accountants could also meet with me there. I would speak to everyone about it when we met that morning.

My plan was to go downstairs and get a workout before showering. It was still dark, and I took a moment to lie still and listen to Katia's soft breathing, the strong longing to hold her close and stay in bed all morning causing me to linger longer than I should. Sighing, I finally eased from the bed, not wanting to wake her. Quickly changing, I went down to the exercise room, had a JKD workout, lifted weights, and went for a quick swim.

After showering and dressing, I went to the kitchen to get a glass of juice and a croissant for Katia. Taking the small breakfast up, I set it on the bedside table along with her pain meds.

"Hi," she said sleepily. I sat down beside her and kissed her brow.

"I didn't mean to wake you, *amore*."

"It's okay. I didn't want to miss you."

"I'm sorry I have to go."

"Don't be sorry. You have to do your job."

"Well, after today I will be holding my meetings here and taking advantage of internet access."

"Really?"

"Yes, that way I am always here, unless there is a major problem at the hotel that I need to take care of. But hopefully there won't be." I caressed her cheek. "Can I do anything else for you?"

She shook her head and smiled. "Just hurry back."

"I will," I promised, lifting her hand to my face, holding it against my cheek.

"Angelo, before you go, I was thinking, how would you feel about me getting Kate to cut my hair?"

Gazing at her gorgeous ringlets splayed over the pillow and shimmering in the early morning light, I said, "I am fine with it." I would miss the long, luxurious locks, but I understood her need to make caring for her hair easier. "You will always look beautiful to me no matter the length of your hair."

She softly caressed my face, letting her thumb brush my lips. I leaned down and touched my mouth to hers. "I love you, my heart."

"I love you."

"Are you sure you will be all right?" I couldn't help worrying.

"I'll be fine, my love. I promise. I will even order some groceries and have them delivered, and I'll make us dinner."

"You don't need to do that. I worry about you overdoing it."

"I want to, Angelo." Her eyes were earnest and imploring. "I need to."

Understanding her need to feel useful and do things for me for as long as she was able, I swallowed back the tears and nodded, wishing my emotions were not always so close to the surface.

"Okay, angel." I kissed her once more. "*Ciao*, Katoosha."

"*Ciao*."

* * *

Katia

Feeling the pain slowly coming on, Katia took her medication with the juice, ate half the croissant, and lay in bed until the pain began to relent. At nine, she called Kate and asked her if she had time to come and cut her hair, hoping she'd caught her at a time that she wasn't suffering from morning sickness. Kate and Lee had called Angelo and Katia the night before to welcome them home and share their news. Kate was finally pregnant again after years of trying. Angelo and Katia were happy for their friends and would not allow sadness over their own inability to have a child diminish their joy.

Kate assured Katia that she was fine this morning and always had time for her. She came right over.

* * *

"What do you think?" Kate asked, handing Katia a mirror when she was done. She had given her a very short, tapered pixie cut.

Katia's eyes moved over the thick tresses covering the floor a moment before gazing at her reflection. "I love it. Do you think Angelo will like it?"

"He will love it," Kate assured her. "Honey, you could have the worst haircut in the world and that man would still think you were the *most beautiful woman* in the world."

Katia smiled. "I still can't believe how much he loves me."

Kate grabbed the broom and started sweeping up the hair. "Angelo's heart was always meant to be yours, Katia."

How thankful she was for that. Blinking tears away, she nodded, brushing a hand over her short hair. "Thank you, Kate."

"You're welcome." She tied a small ribbon around a thick lock of the hair and handed it to Katia, saying softly, "Keep it for Angelo."

Giving Kate a watery smile, Katia accepted the hair. She would place it in a small keepsake box she'd brought back from their honeymoon.

After Kate left, Katia took a quick shower and dressed in a bohemian style skirt and a light, sleeveless crocheted blouse that she'd purchased on Mackinac Island, wanting to look nice for Angelo. Then, putting together a list, she ordered groceries and had them delivered. As soon as she put everything away, she threw together a meatloaf and put it in the oven along with a couple of baked potatoes and set the timer.

By the time she finished, she was so tired, she lay down on the couch in the family room and covered herself with a light blanket, immediately falling asleep.

* * *

I pulled into the driveway, so grateful to finally be home. There had been many things on the agenda during the morning meeting with management and it took longer than normal, which put me behind schedule, making me late for the meeting with the accountants. Before leaving, I made sure everything was in place for conducting future meetings over the internet. I also stopped by the restaurant and grabbed some of Katia's favorite orange cream cake for dessert.

Dinner smelled wonderful as I entered the kitchen.

"Hi," Katia said sleepily, sitting up on the family room couch. Placing the laptop and cake on the counter, I went to her and sat down, immediately taking her in my arms.

I touched her hair, taking a moment to just look at her. She was so beautiful, and the haircut made her striking gray eyes stand out even more.

"Do you like it?" she asked.

"I love it. You're beautiful."

"Thank you."

"How are you?"

"I'm okay, just glad to see you."

Pressing a kiss to her lips, I murmured, "I'm glad to be home again. Now that I'm with you, all is right with the world." She grinned and I kissed her again, warmth rolling through me at the feel of her hands in my hair. She pressed herself against me and I gently tightened my embrace, not wanting to hurt her. She was so fragile to me.

"Angelo," she whispered, parting her

mouth from mine and looking into my eyes, her own imploring, mirroring the desire I was sure she saw in mine.

"Are you sure?"

She nodded, that irresistible smile curving her lips.

"What about dinner?"

"It can wait." She drew my head down, claiming my kiss again, then moved her warm mouth over my jaw, her lips lightly gliding to my neck and I groaned.

"*Si, bella*. It can."

* * *

Later in the night as I lay holding my sweet Katia in my arms, I again relished the feel of her warm breath on my bare skin. I found myself counting those breaths. Each and every one was precious to me. Earlier, I had lain with my head against her heart, listening to each beat, finding comfort in her hands holding me there and her whispered words of love against my ear. I would never take these things for granted. I couldn't. Every moment was everything to me.

She was everything.

Twenty-one

With Every Breath I Breathe
One month later

"It's happening so fast," I said, covering my face with my hands, tears slipping through my fingers.

"I know," Sylvia said, rubbing my back, crying with me. "But think of how long she had been sick and didn't even know. You've had more time with her than many people get. She is a strong and brave woman."

"She is," I agreed, sniffling and wiping my eyes. "I just don't know how I will let her go."

"I can't begin to imagine what you are going through, Angelo, but my heart aches when

I think of her not being in the world. One of the bright lights on this earth is dimming. It will be darker when she is gone, but she will leave a small flame for you, to light your way through this life. Hopefully that flame will grow enough to give you warmth until the day you see her again." She squeezed my hand. "Just remember I will always be here when you need me."

"Thanks, Sylvia, for everything."

We stood and I walked her to the door.

"Call me, no matter the time."

"I will."

Closing the door, I went to the kitchen to get Katia's lunch, which now consisted of nutritional shakes, soup, and organic applesauce because those were the only things she could eat, *when* she ate, and I had to feed her because she was no longer strong enough.

When the pain had worsened even more, the doctor advised me to order a hospital bed for Katia, but she wouldn't hear of it, insisting that she needed to be next to me. I didn't want to sleep away from her either. Her pain medication was increased, so she was asleep most of the time. When she was awake, we didn't talk, we just quietly stared at each other. I could tell there was so much that she wanted to say but didn't have the strength to.

Whenever I had to take care of Katia's personal needs, tears would fill her eyes, and I knew she was saddened that she could not take care of herself. She felt that she was a burden. She didn't have to speak the words because I saw them in her eyes. I would then kiss her mouth, press my lips to her ear and whisper, "I love you so much, *dolcezza*. You are my treasure, and caring for you is never a burden. Please don't think that. This is my place."

Moving to the kitchen window, I gazed out at the back yard, allowing my eyes to travel down to the lake. The view brought to mind the last good day Katia had. It was a few days after we got back from Mackinac. We took a blanket down to the lake where Katia and I lay looking up through the leafy tree limbs at the sky. We talked for a while, sharing memories of the past. Katia moved closer, I drew her into my arms, and became lost in her kiss. She was so warm, her embrace so intoxicating. We whispered our love for each other over and over. Sharing a longing gaze, I carried her back to the house and we made love. It was the last time we were able to share the experience. I thought I would miss it, and I did, but now I missed holding her close to me more.

Drawing my thoughts to the present, I poured the shake into a glass, stuck in a straw and put the glass on a tray along with a small bowl of applesauce. Pausing, I took a moment to get a good handle on my emotions before going up.

Katia was awake.

"Hi, *bella*. I brought you some lunch. Let me sit you up so you can eat." I gently lifted her, doing my best not to cause her additional pain, and placed some pillows behind her back. I sat on the edge of the bed and tried to feed her a spoon of applesauce, but she turned her head away slightly, and I knew she wouldn't be able to eat it. I held the glass and placed the straw between her lips. She was able to take two sips.

"That's good, sweetheart," I said softly. "We will try again in a little while."

Placing the tray on the table, I sat on the bed again and took her hand, startled when she opened her mouth to speak. I leaned over her.

"What is it, my Katia?"

Her voice was just above a whisper. "Adopt a son . . . for us, Angelo. Don't . . . want you . . . be alone." Her eyes were earnest and clearer than they had been for the last week.

"Promise, *amore*."

My dear sweet Katia. She had suffered so much, yet she never stopped thinking of me, never stopped worrying for me. She was the most giving person I knew. Now I would give her this.

"I will," I answered, my voice cracking. "I promise." She slowly smiled then, and I basked in the light of it. I had not thought I would ever see her beautiful smile again in this life.

"Angelo?"

"Yes, my love."

"Would like to . . . lake. Take me?"

"Yes, I will take you."

Wrapping her in a light blanket, I gently scooped her up in my arms and slowly carried her down the path through the back yard, repeatedly kissing her brow on the way. Always small and petite, now she barely weighed seventy pounds. But even with the gaunt features, she was still the most beautiful thing in the world to me.

When we reached the lake, I sat down on the grass and held her on my lap, cradling her in my arms like a child. She slowly opened her eyes, squinting in the bright light. She turned her head slightly, focusing on the lake.

"So beautiful," she whispered.

I had tried to be strong for her, to keep my feelings locked away, but at that moment I couldn't help it. The tears just came in a rush, refusing to be stopped. "You are beautiful," I sobbed, kissing her brow then her lips. "So beautiful. Oh, Katia, I don't know how to be without you."

She turned her eyes to mine, the clarity in them fading. "Live your life, *amore mio*." Her words were slurring together. "Live for both of us . . . Promise."

"I promise." I kissed her again.

She closed her eyes and rested her head against my heart. "Love you."

"I love you too."

"Tell me . . . about our son."

Caressing her face, I gazed out over the lake. In addition to the ducks that normally made their home along our part of the shore, there were a couple of swans that now lived in the lake. They were always there for a short time, showing up for a few months out of the year.

"Our son will be a beautiful boy, a good boy with a good heart. He will take after you that way. He may not share our blood, but with God's help, I will try to teach him the way you would. He will be smart and gifted like you, but I won't ever force him to be creative. Hopefully he will find his gifts on his own.

"I will read to him every day. He will love to read, and he will love doing his schoolwork. We will play ball and I will teach him Jeet Kune Do. We'll go to the park and I will take him to work with me. He'll grow tall and strong and be kind to everyone. And he –"

Hearing Katia's breath catch, I looked down at her closed eyes just as she softly exhaled. Then it happened again, the second slow exhale being her last. And my world immediately stilled.

Clutching her body to me, I sobbed, rocking her slowly.

"And I will teach him about you, Katoosha. I will tell him of the joy you brought to me and how much I loved you, how much I will always love you. He will know you, *amore*. Your posterity will know you and love you as I will forever love you."

Holding my wife tightly against me the way I had not been able to before she took her final breath, I continued to rock her and I wept, my broken sobs echoing in the trees surrounding me.

And in my mind, I could hear her sweet

voice humming the Rhapsody.

Epilogue

Be Seeing You Somewhere in Time

Sitting on a granite bench beside the lake, I cast my line into the water and reel it in a little, my eyes briefly taking in the age spots and spider veins on the backs of my hands that signal old age, for I am indeed old now.

Though I am not looking at them, the words I had engraved on the bench so long ago are also engraved in my heart.

With every breath I breathe I love her,

with longing arms and hands I cling,

too soon arms and hands are empty,

leaving no more breath to breathe.

One day the aroma of her kiss will fill these lungs,

and I will breathe again.

For Katia, My Treasure

It has been fifty years since death separated me and my sweet Katia, and I still wear the ring that ties me to her. It has never come off, and it never will.

I retired from the hotel years ago, and it is now in the hands of our son and his family. I adopted Nick a year after Katia died, keeping my promise to her. He was three years old when I was blessed to become his father and he has brought me great joy, and so has his posterity. *Our posterity.* I had been prepared to not have any once Katia was gone. But she was a wise woman and knew I needed family in order to keep going. She couldn't bear to think of me being alone, and I could not bear to bring her pain by consigning myself to a life of solitude.

With Nick's dark wavy hair and hazel eyes, he could have been born of us, which makes me believe he was meant to be a part of our family all along. I did teach him the best I could and he grew to be a good man. He knows and loves Katia as his mother, and he has said many times that he looks forward to finally meeting her one day. I always tell him that though I long for that for him as well, I hope it will be many years before their meeting.

I have attended church on a regular basis for years now, and I will always be grateful for the two young missionaries that knocked on my door, bringing me the gospel of Jesus Christ. It is the only thing that has helped me get through the years of living without the person who was my other half for so long.

Happily, I can report that I have accomplished all I wanted to in this life and more. I have no regrets. I have loved with my whole heart, and have had that love returned. I truly hope I have made my father, and my Heavenly Father proud.

Now I am eighty-nine years old. My eyesight is fading, my hearing is beginning to diminish, and I look forward to the day I can join my sweet *tesora*, for she was indeed my treasure, the thing I most prized, next to my Savior. My life is winding down and the curtain will one day soon be drawn on this episode of my existence, the final act looming before me, preparing me for my final bow.

Until then, as it has so many times, my mind will go back to another time. I will travel back through the halls of memory where she permanently resides. I see her smile, hear her laughter, and feel her love. I soak in every single detail, allowing myself for a short time to live in that holographic world.

Sometimes during these moments, I hear my sweet Katia's voice and can feel her presence. In those moments, love flows over me, through me.

"Thank you, Katoosha," I always whisper, and I know I am another step closer to feeling her embrace once more. I take comfort in this, and I am grateful for the tender mercy.

One of the last things Katia said to me was, "Live your life, *amore mio*. Live for both of us."

And I have.

* * *

Three years later, surrounded by his family, Angelo died after a short and draining bout of pneumonia. As healthy as he had always been, the family was sure he would recover, but Angelo–and God–had other plans.

As Angelo's spirit separated from his frail,

old body, he opened his eyes, and standing before him in a white Victorian gown with her hand outstretched was his beloved Katia. Her mouth curved in that adorable smile he loved so much, her shining eyes full of love. He cried tears of joy as her arms went around his waist and he clutched her to him, burying his face in her thick, curly tresses and breathing in the fragrance that was her. Then he kissed her, whispering against her lips, "*Ti amo, tesora*. Now I can breathe again."

Because You Loved Me

Katia's Book of Memories

A Til You Come Back to Me Again Extra

I wish I could have known when I was younger just how precious every moment of life is. However, I have learned this truth slowly.

I am nineteen now.

So, I will go back to the beginning and record those precious moments—the good, and the bad.

The pain, the sorrow, the suffering, the beauty, the splendor, the joy.

The love.

"I almost wish we were butterflies and liv'd but three summer days - three such days with you I could fill with more delight than fifty common years could ever contain." **–John Keats**

In the Beginning

Orlando, Florida

Most little girls love fairytales and dream of a fairytale life, complete with a loving, doting mother and father, a fairy godmother, and a dashing prince.

My young mind held no such illusions.

My life was what most people would call a broken one. I was raised by a single mother. She was very beautiful, and many people said she looked like an African goddess with her smooth brown skin and short braids framing her face. I never knew my father or anything about him, only that he was Russian, which is where my name, Ekaterina, came from. Mama and her best friend, Suzanne called me Katia. Suzanne and

Mama were roommates, and were as close as sisters.

Suzanne was equally beautiful in a different way. With her smooth blond hair and sea green eyes, she looked like my Cinderella doll.

When Aunt Suzanne met Angelo De Luca, I was only four years old, and when she brought him home to meet us, I felt like I suddenly had a best friend. He was the successful owner of a five-star hotel and totally alone in the world, having lost his father the year before.

During the time Angelo and Aunt Suzanne were dating, he would sometimes babysit me while Mama and Suzanne hung out. He usually took me shopping and out for treats and always brought me back home with new clothes or toys. I loved my time with Angelo because he made me feel loved, and he always called to say hello and ask me how I was. He really was my best friend, like the father or older brother I never had. When he and Suzanne married, I was the flower girl at their wedding. Angelo called me his little princess and I was so happy. Their marriage meant he would always be a part of mine and Mama's life.

Drugs and alcohol. Those words were

foreign to a four-year-old, but I was aware enough to know they had always been present in my home. Those two things seemed to make Mama and Suzanne happy, which made me happy.

I had no clue, however, just how destructive those things were until two years later. That lesson came the day I found Mama lying on her bedroom floor. I had tried to cook a pack of noodles and burned myself when I spilled boiling water on my arm. It was painful and I cried as I went to find Mama. She was unconscious on the floor next to her bed, her head resting in a puddle of vomit. Despite my cries and attempts to wake her, she never moved. Mama had told me the day before that she was sick, and she was going away for a while to get better. She said I would stay with Angelo and Suzanne.

When Angelo and Suzanne got there, Suzanne screamed and cried over Mama's body. Angelo picked me up and held me while he called for help. But there was nothing the paramedics could do. Mama was gone.

Angelo rode in the ambulance with me and held me in the emergency room while the doctor treated my burn, and I burrowed against his chest, crying. I was afraid, and he and Suzanne were all I had left. Afterward, we went back to get some of my things. Angelo had me wait in the car. He could tell I was afraid, so he kissed my forehead and promised he would be right back. He ran inside and was back a few minutes later.

When we reached his home (and now my home as well) Angelo carried me and my sack of clothing into the big beautiful house. I clung to his neck, never wanting to let him go. Because of bad dreams, he ended up rocking me that night until I cried myself to sleep. There would be many nights like that.

Sadly, through the next few years, Suzanne's drinking worsened. She was never the same after Mama's death, and Angelo and Suzanne's marriage continued to crumble.

Some people would say my life was better, and in many ways, it was. But sadly, I had just been taken from one tragic situation and put into another.

I had heard that time is a healer. I guess only time would tell.

Broken

Six Years Later

It was another day at work with Angelo. He had meetings all morning at the hotel, so we didn't see Suzanne. She was still in bed when we left. She usually was. Many times, she stayed in her pajamas and drank the day away, which was really sad.

When I came to stay with Angelo and Suzanne, Angelo decided to teach me at home. From the very beginning, Suzanne never participated in my education. She always said she was too busy, and it saddened me that she never gave me attention. She was the only mother I had now, but I guess it didn't really matter to her.

I was ten now, and when Angelo had

meetings, I usually went with him. I would sit in his office and quietly do my work.

I learned so much from Angelo, and I don't know why, but learning quickly became a need for me. I needed to take in everything and I couldn't seem to stop. In addition to my school studies, Angelo taught me to play the piano and I practiced for an hour each day, sometimes longer, wanting to play as well as he did. We soon began to play duets. He always told me how proud he was of me, which made me happy because he was happy.

Angelo had studied martial arts for years, and one day I asked him to teach me. He told me it was actually Jeet Kune Do and explained exactly what it was and what was involved.

"As I explained to Suzanne years ago, Jeet Kune Do is a martial arts system that encompasses physical, scientific, mental, social, and spiritual knowledge. It's completely different from the other forms of martial arts."

"What do you mean?" I had asked.

"Well, it is all about using minimal movements and extreme speed to gain maximum effects. It's a set of tools that you use for different situations. Bruce Lee was the Jeet Kune Do master, and he said that the perfect style was no style, and you can use something from everything. You use what works and throw everything else away. He didn't like formalistic fighting, which is what most forms of martial arts are about. It makes sense." He had grinned at me. "But it doesn't make sense to you, does it?"

"No," I had answered, "but I still want to learn."

He just chuckled and hugged me, and I knew he would agree. So, he began giving me instruction and told me he was blown away by how fast I learned. Well immersed in the art, I soon moved on, needing to add something else.

After watching a concert on television one evening, the next day I asked Angelo if I could learn the cello.

"Are you sure?" he asked me.

"Yes, I really want to learn."

He bought me a student cello, hired a teacher and I started lessons. Studying and practicing hard, I picked it up quickly. I immediately moved on to the violin and the guitar, and Angelo turned one of the extra bedrooms into a music room for me. My instruments stood in every corner, and framed posters of great musicians hung on the walls.

A few months before I turned nine, I

wanted to start studying ballet. Angelo didn't bother asking me if I was sure. He enrolled me in a class one afternoon a week. I advanced quickly and was now en pointe. He had floor to ceiling mirrors and a barre installed in the vacant game room. The room already had a hardwood floor, and I now used it to practice three times a week. Angelo said he was completely amazed by me. He called me a prodigy and always showered me with praise. He encouraged me in everything I wanted to do. It was one of the things I loved about him. He had no idea that this was how I coped. To keep from thinking about my mother, I needed to focus on other things. This is something I did not truly understand until I was older. I needed stability, and it seemed Angelo was now the only permanent fixture in my life.

While Angelo sat at his desk with Tim and Andrew, I worked in my spelling book. Sensing his gaze, I looked up and smiled. Having learned some sign language online, I lifted my hands and signed, "I love you, Angelo."

Grinning, he signed back, "I love you, too, *tesora mia*." He always called me his little treasure.

* * *

Angelo finished his meeting by two. After

the men left, he packed up his laptop and helped me pack up my things.

"What do you say we call Suzanne and see if she wants to go out and eat with us?"

"Okay. Can I call her?"

"Sure."

He gave me his cell and I dialed. I knew there was a good chance she would say no, but there was always hope. I still loved Suzanne and I really missed the days that she loved me too. The phone continued to ring, then it went to voicemail.

"No answer at home," I finally said. "Should I try her cell?"

"Yes. If she's out already, maybe we can meet her."

While I called, I watched Angelo look over his appointment book and check his schedule for the next week. He closed it, his eyes growing distant, and he suddenly looked tired, and sad.

"Who is this?" I asked when a male voice answered. Then I heard familiar laughter and Suzanne's voice saying, to the man, "Come back to bed." I immediately hung up and handed Angelo the phone.

"What is it?" he asked, the sadness in his eyes deepening.

"A man answered and . . ."

"And what?" he said, pressing a hand to my cheek. "It's all right, sweetheart, you can tell me."

Tears rolled down my face, my young heart breaking. "Angelo, she was laughing and told him to . . . come back to bed." I started crying and Angelo held me as I buried my face against his shoulder. I was young, but I knew what I heard. I couldn't believe Suzanne could do this to him. To us.

"It's all right, *tesorina*," he whispered into my hair as I clung to him. "Everything is going to be all right." He kissed my brow. "Let's go home. We'll stop and get something on the way."

Hurt

We were sitting at the dining room table when the phone rang, and Angelo got up to answer it. We had gotten pizza on the way home, but I was no longer hungry. I had lost my appetite, still upset by the earlier call.

"I am going to the den to talk a moment," he said, kissing my brow. "I'll be back." I nodded and watched him walk away, my heart aching thinking about how hurt he must be.

I put the remaining pizza in a container and placed it in the refrigerator. Then I wiped off the table and went to my room. Sitting on my bed, I drew my legs up and pressed my face against my bent knees, pondering our situation. Truthfully, I didn't know what to think anymore.

With one phone call, my world had been turned upside down yet again. Angelo hadn't seemed surprised at all, it had just been a confirmation of what looked to be the finality of their marriage. I never knew my heart could hurt so much.

A long while later, Angelo came in and sat down. He opened his arms and I moved into them.

"She doesn't love us anymore," I murmured, my face buried in his shirt.

"Oh, *piccola,* she is just sick right now. Her drinking is a sickness and she needs help."

"Why won't she let us help her? We could."

"I know, sweetheart. I want to, but she needs more help than we can give her."

"We can pray."

"You are right. Let's do that right now. Would you like me to say it or would you like to?"

"I will."

I never knew how to pray until coming to live with Angelo. He taught me how, and now I never missed a night of prayer because I knew how important it was to God to hear from me. Angelo taught me that, too.

We knelt beside my bed and I took a

moment to ponder what I wanted to say. When I finally began, the words that came to my mind were few.

"Please, God, help Suzanne to know we love her. Help her to not hurt anymore. In Jesus's name, amen." I looked up at Angelo. "Was that okay?"

"That was perfect." He hugged me and left me to change into my pajamas. A few minutes later, he came back and tucked me in. It was still early, but my heart was tired and I just wanted to sleep. Angelo kissed me and sat with me for a little while until I drifted off.

* * *

A short time later I awoke to the sound of sirens and I looked out my bedroom window. At the sight of the ambulance, I jumped up and raced down the stairs, yelling Angelo's name. I moved to the open doorway and he turned and caught me up in his arms, turning me away just as the paramedics were pulling Suzanne from the taxi. Just that brief glimpse of her still body was enough to traumatize me. I wrapped my arms around his neck and cried. It was happening again. It was Mama all over again. As Angelo held me, I heard him crying too. It was like a bad dream I couldn't seem to wake up from. And I wondered if I would ever be able to sleep again.

* * *

The next day, because he could not lie to me, Angelo told me what happened.

He said the cause of Suzanne's death was an overdose. Her heart stopped. It just finally gave out. She simply went to sleep and never woke up.

* * *

Three days later, we stood beside her grave, staring at the bronze, carnation-draped casket hovering over the waiting hole in the earth. We were alone now. Everyone else had left after offering their condolences and heartfelt words of comfort. Suzanne's parents had been the last to say goodbye. They had hugged us and promised to always be there when we needed them.

Watching them walk away, I told myself I would never need anyone but Angelo, and I begged God to never take him away from me.

This graveside service had been no different from my mother's. Both women had been troubled and lost, at least that's what I heard someone whisper during the service. Their words didn't make me angry, only sad because they were true. As young as I was, even I could see that.

As Angelo slipped on his sunglasses, tightened his hand around mine, and we walked back to the waiting limo, I realized that, in a different way, we were lost now too.

Healing Heart

Six months later

"Angelo!" I cried, waking from another nightmare, and he was instantly there.

"I'm here, *piccola*," he whispered. "I'm here." He lay beside me and I burrowed against him. The vision of the paramedics pulling Suzanne's body from the taxi was still as fresh and vivid as ever. It was always followed by the vision of Angelo standing in front of me slowly fading away, his face wearing a sad, haunted smile.

"I don't want you to leave me, Angelo," I said, whimpering, too afraid to close my eyes again. "I'm so scared I will lose you too."

"Shhh, I promise I will never leave you,

Katoosha. I promise I will always be here. Shhh, it's all right. It's okay, *tesora mia*."

He crooned those words over and over until I drifted back to sleep. The nightmares only happened once or twice a week now, less than before. I was slowly getting better. I was starting to feel more secure.

Soon, the dreams stopped completely.

* * *

Sometimes I missed Suzanne, and I knew Angelo did too. Emotionally, she had not been there for a long time, but we still missed her. On those days, the sadness was deeply etched in Angelo's expression and it made me even sadder. He told me he sometimes wondered if he'd done all he could to help Suzanne. He wondered if he'd been good enough to her, if he'd loved her enough, if he'd been a good enough husband to her. There were times that his sadness was so consuming, I began to pray to God for a way to help him. The answer was always the same. I would go to him, hug his neck, kiss his cheek and say, "I love you, Angelo. You're the best person in the world," because he was. He would smile and hug me, and the fog would lift again.

"I love you too, *tesorina*," he always said.

I usually went with Angelo on his fishing

days with Lee and Kate. I loved spending time with them and I absolutely loved to fish. There was something very calming about casting my line in the water and patiently waiting for a bite. I loved everything about it, from baiting my own hook to reeling in and unhooking my catch.

Lee and Kate were always so good to me, and Kate usually brought me a special treat. They were good people and I was happy that they were such good friends to Angelo, because he really needed friends. Kate had been unable to have a child and she just found out she was pregnant. We were so happy for them. It made me sad to think of them never having the opportunity to be parents, because I knew they would be great ones. Their child would be lucky to have them.

Angelo and I spent a lot of time down by the lake. We would sit on the grassy bank and talk about a variety of things–movies, books, things he did when he was a boy. He told me about losing his mother in a car accident, and I always touched the scar just at his hairline, a result of the accident. His hair covered it so you couldn't tell. He talked about moving from Italy and about losing his father to cancer. We talked about the hotel and he shared his experiences working with his father.

"Do you still miss him?" I asked one afternoon as I tossed bits of bread out to the ducks.

"Every day."

I thought about that for a moment. "Do you think he would like me?"

"He would love you as much as I do."

I grinned. "How much do you love me?"

"Hmmm, let me think. Well, do you know how big the universe is?"

"Nobody does. It's endless, like it goes on forever."

"And that is how much I love you."

A happy warmth filled me and I crawled into his lap. I was pretty small for my age and he always seemed like a giant to me. "That's how much I love you too."

Smiling, he kissed my nose and hugged me close, pressing his nose into my hair. "Thank you, *passerotta*."

* * *

A few weeks before I turned eleven, I decided that I wanted to have a birthday party and invite the neighborhood kids. There were only about ten kids that were near or around my age and I didn't know any of them that well. I knew I needed to get to know more people and that was now my goal.

"It's about time I got to know them," I told Angelo.

He smiled, studying my expression and I knew I must have been wearing what he called my "serious look."

"You know you have the most expressive eyes I have ever seen on anyone your age, and the gray seems to deepen every year."

I knew what he said was true. I studied my reflection occasionally and had seen the changes. My eyes were almond shaped and framed by thick, dark lashes, the kind of lashes Angelo told me many women would pay a fortune for. I noticed that my voice had also deepened slightly, the tone of it a little raspy. It made me sound older than I was, which I didn't mind at all. My hair had grown so much that it reached the middle of her back. I usually kept it pulled back in a loose ponytail. I remember how hard a time Angelo had brushing and styling my hair when I was younger. Sylvia finally taught him how. My curly mane had been especially thick, which made it even trickier to work with. Sadly, Suzanne had never been much help either. Before she and Angelo married, she had helped

Mama out by doing my hair occasionally. After marriage, that changed, just like everything else. When I turned eight, Angelo began teaching me to care for my own hair and I managed to catch on quickly.

"So, you are ready for some socializing, huh?" Angelo asked. We were sitting at the table eating ice-cream bars.

"Yeah. I've put it off for too long."

He chuckled. "Well, I don't know. I might have to give this some thought. We can't have you turning into a socialite just yet. You will only be eleven."

Placing my hands on my hips, I gave him 'the look.' "Angelo De Luca! If you don't stop –"

"Okay!" he said, throwing his hands up. I knew he secretly loved it when I turned into 'Little Miss Assertive,' and he always tried not to laugh until I did, which usually didn't take long. "I will be happy to fund your grand soiree."

"Thank you."

"I guess we should make a list of people to invite and go shopping. Do you know what kind of cake you would like?"

"Not really." I hadn't really thought about it until he mentioned it.

"All right, we will look around. When you

decide on a theme we can work on the cake."

"Okay." I quickly made up a guest list, making sure to add Sylvia because she was such a neat lady, and I loved her because she was so good to Angelo.

When the list was finished, we went to the party supply store. I browsed around a bit and finally decided that I wanted the party to be a luau.

"Are you sure?" Angelo asked with a surprised smile. "I kind of thought you would choose a Barbie theme or one of the popular boy bands you kids are so crazy over."

"No, I wanted to choose something fun that everyone will enjoy. Besides, I don't really like that kind of music anyway."

"I know," he said, giving my hair a gentle tug. "I was just teasing my classical, bluesy girl."

"You know it," I said and he laughed.

We bought all the decorations and various items we would need for the party, including a tiki piñata and enough candy to fill it. Then Angelo took me to the bakery and ordered a large, two-layer sheet cake, decorated with tropical flowers, hula dancers, and mini surfboards. For the food, we wanted to keep with the theme, so we decided on pulled pork sliders, deli chips and pineapple punch.

After our shopping, Angelo took me to my favorite Chinese restaurant for dinner. We talked more about the party and I planned the games. Angelo just smiled, listening to me go on about how much fun it would be. His smile was because he loved seeing me happy. He never needed to tell me my happiness was the most important thing in the world to him. He never needed to say the words because I knew, just as I knew there was nothing he would not do for me. He would give me the moon if he could. The fact is, he already had. I had everything.

Changes

On the day of the party, I wasn't feeling very well. I had been excited all week and had really looked forward to this party, but from the time I woke up that morning, I felt off somehow. Angelo noticed my somber mood and asked me if I was okay. Not wanting him to worry, I assured him that I was.

Sylvia came earlier in the day and helped us decorate the back patio. Angelo picked up the order of mini buns and pulled pork, and Sylvia helped us make the sandwiches. After we finished, I went to change while Angelo made the punch.

Soon the guests started arriving, each bringing a gift. I thanked each person for coming.

Most of the kids there I had only come in contact with once or twice, so I was really looking forward to getting to know everyone. I briefly glanced down at my outfit, hoping I looked okay. I had chosen to wear a peach sundress with my curls pulled up away from my face, cascading down my back. I had tucked a yellow flower in my hair that matched the lei hanging around my neck.

I smiled at Angelo as he stood by, looking on like a proud papa as I entertained and mingled. We played some games, ate, and took turns whacking at the piñata. Jared, a boy that I invited, and who followed me around a lot, finally broke it. He seemed really nice, but his hovering kind of creeped me out a little.

We all scrambled around, picking up candy. Then I opened my gifts. I received clothing, jewelry, and gift cards. Sylvia gave me an art set, which I loved. I looked forward to using it and expanding my creativity.

I saved Angelo's gift for last. Because he knew me so well, I knew his gift would be something that came from his heart. Unwrapping the package and opening the box, I smiled and cried, "Oh, Angelo!" In the box was a book about Bruce Lee, a book of show tunes sheet music, a little pair of diamond earrings along with a gift certificate for ear piercing, and a framed photo of us that Sylvia had taken the month before during one of Angelo's meetings. I was sitting next to Angelo behind the desk, looking over some papers. We were laughing and joking about me taking over his job. It was a priceless picture, one that meant everything to me.

Throwing my arms around his neck, I kissed his cheek, whispering, "This was the best gift ever," and he hugged me tightly. The whole gift was awesome, but for me, the photo represented stability, another sign that he would never abandon me.

After playing another game, we moved the party to the pool, but I didn't feel like swimming. Plus, my stomach had started to hurt a little. I sat with another girl and just talked and watched the others. Twice, Jared winked at me before diving in, earning a raised brow and a grin from Angelo. When I gave him a saucy look in return, he chuckled and kiss my cheek, leaving me to go grab more sandwiches for my guests.

A little over an hour later, they were done swimming and Angelo helped everyone locate their clothes among the piles lying by the pool and handed out towels. Everyone thanked me for inviting them and I thanked them all once more for the gifts.

After the party was over and everyone had gone, I took the gifts to my room. I had planned on going back down and helping Angelo and Sylvia clean up, but my stomachache got worse and something suddenly did not feel right. I felt sick. Thinking I might throw up, I quickly went to the bathroom, startled by what I found. Leaning over the sink for a moment, I drank a little water before going back into my room. I lay down on my bed and curled up, holding my stomach. That was the way Angelo found me a while later. By then I hurt so bad, I was in tears. I had never felt anything like it before.

Angelo sat down next to me. "Katia, what is it, *tesorina*?"

"It hurts."

"What hurts, *piccola*?"

"My stomach."

He pressed the back of his hand to my forehead and cheek. "Do you feel sick?"

"A little."

"Maybe you ate a little too much."

"But I hardly ate anything. And Angelo . . . there was blood . . . when I went to the bathroom."

For a moment, his eyes widened slightly, but then his expression quickly calmed. He caressed my cheek. "Do you think you can get up to change into your pajamas?"

"Yes, but . . ."

"Just lie here for a bit. I'll be right back, all right?"

"Okay."

He kissed my brow, whispering. "Be right back, Katoosha."

* * *

He returned a few minutes later, his hands full. Sitting on the side of my bed again, he handed me a dose of pain medicine. Then he placed a pack of sanitary napkins on my bedside table (Suzanne had purchased a supply) and patiently explained what was happening. He explained about menstruation, told me about a woman's reproductive system, and how my body was changing and preparing for womanhood. After asking some questions, I understood. He explained how to use the feminine products. I figured many girls would probably be embarrassed by having to discuss this with an adult, but I wasn't. This was Angelo, the person I loved most in the world. I could talk to him about anything.

I went to change and got into bed. I was still in pain, but it was starting to ease up a bit. As I closed my eyes, Angelo tucked the covers around me and sat with me for a bit, gently brushing the hair back from my face, caressing my brow. His touch was soothing, and as the room darkened, I finally drifted off to his whispered, "*Ti amo*, my Katia."

* * *

As I got older, Kate began taking me on girl shopping trips. She helped me pick out things I needed, and would yet need, as my body changed–things I should have had a mother helping me with. Angelo tried, but I knew there was so much he was still learning when it came to raising me. Taking care of a boy was one thing, but girls are an entirely different species. Even I knew that.

I sometimes had mood shifts, but not as many as the average girl. Angelo always said there was nothing average about me. Sometimes I looked at other kids my age and wondered if I was normal at all. But after seeing the way some interacted with their families, I would take being abnormal any day. I loved Angelo too much to ever be disrespectful to him in any way. There were only two times that my hormones ran high and I had bad moments. Those moments were awful and I hated it because I knew how much it hurt Angelo that I wouldn't talk to him, and we had always been able to talk about anything. Both times I cried and apologized the next day. His forgiveness was instant and he took me out for ice-cream. He always knew the way to my heart.

I started taking over the cooking. Armed with an American-Italian cookbook, I became a pretty good cook and he gladly turned the kitchen over to me. He even bought me a couple of chef aprons–one red and one yellow, my two favorite colors–and a plaque to hang on the wall that said, **Katia's Kitchen**. Many times, we would cook together, even making a few of the dishes on the hotel restaurant menu.

I sometimes had sleepovers at Sylvia's place. Since Sylvia never had children of her own, she kind of adopted me, and I loved spending time with her. She always had fun things planned. Sometimes Kate joined us and we made it a regular slumber party. Angelo always said I came back still giddy from the time I shared with them, and I suppose he was right. A night with the girls was always fun and definitely a learning experience. Because of them, I was slowly learning how to be a lady.

* * *

Once a month, Angelo and I volunteered in the soup kitchen at the homeless shelter. I loved seeing familiar and new faces, dishing out food, and serving. True, most teens would have probably found it boring, but not me. I would rather spend time there with Angelo, serving others than anywhere else. I did hang out a little with friends and had expanded my social circle, but I still preferred doing things with Angelo. After all, he was all the family I had.

Sometimes we went to the residential part of the shelter and visited with the children, spending time reading to them or playing games. The families loved any attention their children could get, and we always came away wishing we could do more. We made donations and kept them all in our prayers.

Angelo even let me hold a bake sale in the yard to raise money and we put together fun care packages for the children. He supported and encouraged me in everything I did, and that meant more than I could ever say.

* * *

I continued to learn new thing whenever I could, which kept me from having too many idle moments. Angelo said I must have been born with a driven spirit and that my brain never shut off during waking moments, and I possessed a burning need to learn everything I possibly could. Maybe he was right.

I liked to sing whenever I was alone in the house. One day I found a free singing program online designed to help people improve their singing voice, and I began practicing whenever Angelo was out. Since I was usually with him most of the time, the opportunities were sparse. One day when I had more time, I would pick it up again. Singing made me feel good, and I hoped that one day I would be brave enough to let Angelo hear me.

* * *

When I turned fifteen, I finished school, having taken the SAT and the ACT and passing both with perfect scores. Angelo said this was a major feat, and he was proud of me. He said I had come farther and accomplished more than he ever dreamed, and to reward me for doing so well, we took a trip to Italy and Greece. We had taken many trips through the years, but never out of the country.

It was an amazing experience for me. We spent the first few days in Rome, seeing the sights–the coliseum, museums, ancient churches and basilicas–and visiting with people Angelo knew growing up. He took me by his old home. The people living in the lovely villa were friendly and allowed us to come inside so Angelo could show me around. It wasn't hard picturing him as a small boy roaming the halls there.

We shared a few meals with two families he knew well and I discovered that dinner time in Italian families is always a major event. Since all the grown children lived in the same area, they shared dinner each day. Thanks to Angelo's lessons through the years, I was fluent in Italian and could follow the conversations easily, despite how rapidly they spoke.

We spent two days in Treviso, two days in Milan–the shopping capitol–a day in Verona, and our last two days in Venice, saving it for last. Though I was used to living by a lake, waking to the view of the Grand Canal was a totally new and unique experience.

Just as in the other cities, we filled the days in Venice shopping and touring the old churches, including the most famous church, St. Mark's Basilica. Both evenings, we took a gondola ride down the canal. Venice during the day was pretty cool, but at night it was amazing! Everything was lit up like Christmas.

On our final night in Italy, we stood on the Rialto Bridge. It was late so it wasn't as crowded. Angelo knew I wanted to take in every last moment, so he allowed me to linger. As we stood watching the gondoliers steering late night passengers beneath us, I felt a lingering sense of awe. This trip was a dream come true for me and I was filled with gratitude.

"Thank you for bringing me, Angelo," I said.

He wrapped an arm around my shoulders and smiled. "You are very welcome. I'm so happy I could share the country of my birth with you." He sighed, hugging me close. "No matter how long I live in America, Italy will always be home."

I looked up at him, watching melancholy fill his expression.

"Do you miss living here?"

"Always. But coming back makes me not so homesick."

"Can we come back again sometime?" I grinned. "After all, we do have to make sure you don't get homesick."

He laughed. "Thank you for being so concerned for my welfare."

"I do my best."

He chuckled. "*Si, tesora mia.* We will come back sometime."

The Caribbean

When I turned sixteen, Angelo planned a Caribbean cruise vacation for my birthday. He said he had always wanted to go on a cruise, and when he told me what he had planned, I was ecstatic. In fact, I was so excited, I insisted we take a Latin dance class. It was fun and Angelo was the perfect partner. I was sure his Italian blood gave him his rhythm.

A couple of days before we were scheduled to leave, I had three girlfriends over to share some of my chocolate birthday cake, and they brought gifts. They were my best friends and I really appreciated their friendship. Kimberly, Alison and Denise were fellow ballet students and they sometimes came over to put in a little extra practice with me, especially when there was an upcoming recital. While I was now finished with school, they were starting their junior year. When I passed my tests, I had wondered if things would be awkward between us since we would no longer have school in common. But it wasn't awkward at all, and they actually envied me for being done. We were so close I didn't think anything would ever change between us.

Two days later, we flew to San Juan, Puerto Rico and boarded the ship there. Angelo had gotten us suites next to each other. Since we would not set sail until ten that night, we put our carry-on bags in our rooms and went back off the ship. We walked across the street to a pharmacy and bought bottled water to take on the cruise. Since we planned to spend a couple of days in San Juan when we got back, we decided the sightseeing could wait and just went back to the ship.

After putting the water in our rooms, we walked around the ship and got familiar with the layout before heading to the Lido deck to have dinner. Grabbing a burger and fries from the grill and salad and dessert from the nearby buffet, we sat at one of the tables out on deck and ate. There was a live band playing island music. It was all so festive, I was positively giddy. Angelo glanced over at me and laughed.

"Are you having a good time, Katoosha?"

"Definitely! And we haven't even left the port."

He laughed again, taking it all in as well. "I wish we weren't leaving so late. I wanted to watch the deportation. But I guess we will have plenty of other opportunities to do that."

"I know," I said. "And just think, tomorrow we will wake up in St. Thomas. I'm so excited!"

"Really? I can't tell at all." I gave him my signature smirk and he grinned.

When we finished our meal, I grabbed his hand. "Let's go, Angelo. I want to go look in the shop windows."

"Already making plans for my money, huh?" I smiled widely and he chuckled. "Oh, all right, let's go."

As we walked through the pool area, we passed by two boys that looked to be my age. They smiled and I smiled back. One was tall with short red hair and freckles, the other, a little taller than me with bleach-blond hair and dimples. They were the same two guys I had seen earlier when we were boarding. I glanced back at Angelo and he shook his head, laughing. He had joked with me earlier about gaining a swarm of admirers on the cruise. His arched brow clearly said, "See, it's starting already." Truthfully, I didn't really see anything special about myself. At four-foot-four inches, I now had a womanly body, toned by years of dance and martial arts. My hair was long, thick and curly. I noticed guys staring every once in a while, but I still didn't think there was anything spectacular about me.

The ship shops would not be open until we were out at sea, so we leisurely browsed the merchandise in the windows. I made a mental note of the things I really wanted, knowing that Angelo would buy them for me. He had always been the most giving person I knew.

Later that evening after our luggage was delivered and we had unpacked, we went to our assigned muster station for the safety drill. Since the ship would be departing soon, we decided to sit out on deck and wait. Then the foghorn sounded and we slowly sailed out.

* * *

I knocked on Angelo's door bright and early the next morning. He was running the electric razor over his face when he opened the door.

"Good morning, *tesorina*. I will only be a moment."

"That's okay, I know I'm early." I sat on the couch and waited while he put his sandals on. "Angelo, your hair is still dripping wet." I grabbed a towel and gently dried it.

He shrugged, glancing at the wet spots on his shirt. I loved his hair. It was thick and reached past his collar. I remembered Suzanne complaining about the length of his hair, and I was secretly glad he never cut it.

He smiled. "I was trying to hurry because I knew a certain young lady would be eager to go."

Grinning, I kissed his cheek. "Thank you. Okay, let's go."

Chuckling at my impatience, he grabbed his wallet and room key, slipping his camera and passport into my tote bag.

"All right, let's go, Miss Adventure Seeker."

We went to the buffet and ate a quick breakfast before heading down to the lower level to disembark.

* * *

We started by taking an open-air tour bus

around St. Thomas. It was a beautiful island, too incredible for words. As we rode through the narrow mountain roads, we snapped photos of the tropical plants and trees. The island people were very hospitable and waved as buses rolled by, making us all feel welcome and at home.

The bus driver dropped us and a few others off in the historic district, agreeing to come back and pick us up in a while. We visited Fort Christian, the Historical Trust Museum, the Emancipation Gardens, and toured the St. Thomas Synagogue, taking plenty of pictures along the way.

When we approached the famous 99 Steps (the brochure said it was actually one-hundred-three steps) I grinned, excitement filling me. At the top was another set of steps leading to Blackbeard's Castle. "Are you ready?" I asked Angelo and he chuckled.

"Lead the way, *tesora*."

We then started up the steps. When we reached the top of the second set of steps, we stood at the Danish watchtower known as Blackbeard's Castle. I took pictures of the pirate statues as we toured the grounds, and then Angelo took photos of the view from the top of the tower. A tourist asked if we would like him to take our picture and we said yes.

We bought some t-shirts in the castle gift shop, including a pink one for Sylvia because it was her favorite color.

"Was it worth it?" Angelo asked me as we made our way back down the steps.

"It was." I wrapped my arm around his. "Thanks."

"You're welcome."

We caught the tour bus back the port, stopping for a moment to listen to some live island music. Angelo put a few dollars in the donation can on the ground in front of the group. They gave us a wave of thanks as we walked away. We stopped by a few shops for more souvenirs before going back to the ship.

* * *

We had dinner in the formal dining room, sharing a table with six other people. There were two couples, and a mother and daughter who were seated next to us. We started out complete strangers, but we soon got to know each other a little. The woman sat next to Angelo. Her name was Cara and she was a single mother. Her daughter Shaylee was my age. Cara was pretty and Shaylee looked just like her.

Shaylee and I talked quite a bit while the

adults conversed around us. Since the next day would be a sea day, she and I made plans to spend some time together at Club 02, a club room where teens fifteen to seventeen participated in fun activities or just hung out. I was happy to have made a friend.

After dinner, Angelo took me to the shop area, and though there were some things I wanted, I decided to wait for the sales before buying anything. Angelo hugged me and said he was proud of me for being frugal. I had always been that way and would much rather shop for bargains than pay full price for anything.

After stopping by the rooms for a bit to freshen up, we went to watch a variety show. We ran into Cara and Shaylee and invited them to sit with us. Cara took a seat next to Angelo and Shaylee sat by me so we could talk while waiting for the show to start. We discussed the activities the club crew had planned for our age group and were excited to go. Angelo and Cara also chatted until the show started.

Just before the lights dimmed, Shaylee leaned over and whispered to me, "My mom thinks your dad is hot."

I looked at her and something immediately shifted inside me, an unfamiliar pain clinching my insides. Shaking my head slightly and swallowing hard, I gave her a small smile and turned my eyes to the stage.

The magician performing was also a comedian. I had been excited because I loved magic and comedy, and the combination was bound to be good. And he *was* good. But I couldn't get into it. I couldn't even laugh.

"Are you okay?" Angelo whispered, squeezing my hand. I quickly grinned.

"Yes, I'm good."

"Are you sure?"

I nodded, my smile widening, which took more effort than it should have. "I am, really."

I noticed Angelo frequently glancing my way throughout the performance. I forced myself to laugh in the appropriate places, hoping I sounded genuine. Once when I caught him looking at me, I wrapped my arm around his and rested my head on his shoulder, closing my eyes as he pressed a kiss to my brow.

After the show, Angelo thanked Cara and Shaylee for sitting with us and wished them a good night. Shaylee told me she would see me tomorrow, but I wasn't looking forward to it as much as I had been earlier.

When we reached our rooms, Angelo

asked me again if I was okay. He had always been more perceptive to my feelings than I wanted and I could usually mask them well enough. So why not now?

I told him I was just tired and hugged him, kissing his cheek.

"Goodnight, Angelo. See you in the morning."

"Goodnight, *tesorina.*"

"I promise I'm fine. Promise me you won't worry."

He smiled, cupping my cheek. "But that's my job."

"And you're so good at it." I smirked and he chuckled.

"All right," he said. "See you in the morning."

* * *

I stood in front of the balcony doors and watched the moon's light reflect off the ocean waves. The day had been perfect. How could I let one remark bring me down and spoil my evening? Everything had been fine until Shaylee leaned over during the show and said, "My mom thinks your dad is hot." Her words affected me deeply. I didn't like the idea of Cara being attracted to Angelo. Ever since Suzanne broke his heart, I'd felt protective of Angelo. I didn't want him to ever be hurt again. But I also knew he deserved to be happy.

Still, it had been just the two of us for so long, I always felt that Angelo was mine alone, and I was not ready to share him with anyone else. I didn't know if I ever would be.

What is wrong with me? I knew I needed to snap out of this and get over my selfishness.

And I will, I vowed.

I will be better tomorrow.

Jewel Adams

Working at Normal

After showering and readying myself for the day, I knelt and said my prayers. Then I sat on the bed for a moment, psyching myself up for the day. The rest of our vacation would be amazing. I was determined to make it amazing, which meant no more selfish thinking for me.

Having given myself a sufficient pep talk, I grabbed my key and left my room.

As soon as I knocked, the door opened.

"Good morning," Angelo said, drawing me into a hug.

"Good morning." I moved back and gifted him with a genuine smile, letting him know I was back to my normal self. "Are you ready?"

"Just let me grab my key."

* * *

After breakfast and another jaunt around the ship, Angelo and I put on our swimsuits and went up to the pool. There were so many people, we couldn't really swim. After a few minutes of floating in one spot, we got out and went up to sit in the hot tub. It was vacant, so we had it all to ourselves. We stayed in for fifteen minutes or so, then we lay out and dried in the sun.

As we were heading back to our rooms, we ran into Cara and Shaylee. I told Shaylee I would meet her at Club O2 after I changed. Since we were going to be hanging out for a while, Cara invited Angelo to go up and play a game of ping pong and I quickly encouraged him to go. He needed to do something fun while I was out.

When we got to Club 02, there was a group of teens participating in karaoke and another sitting around talking. Since the latter group was mainly guys, Shaylee made a beeline toward their table and I dutifully followed. They anxiously made room for us and each person introduce himself. The two girls said hello then went to join the karaoke group. With their departure, we were immediately made the center of attention. Shaylee reveled in the attention. I didn't. My mind was actually on another part of the ship with Angelo. I wondered if he was having fun with Cara. I wondered what they were talking about. I wondered if she was making him laugh.

I wondered why I cared.

Get a life, Ekaterina! The fact that my mind felt the need to scream this was a sure sign that there was definitely something wrong with me.

* * *

It was the first of two formal dress nights. Angelo had finished dressing before me and was soon knocking on my door. I quickly opened it and rushed back to the sofa to put on my shoes.

"I can't believe you beat me," I said in a playful huff.

"I can't either. But then again, women always need more time when it comes to playing dress up."

"You're right about that," I said, finally standing.

He whistled. "Wow, *bella*! You look incredible."

My face warmed and I looked down at myself. I was wearing a long-sleeve black gown. The top had a mandarin collar with silver woven through the material. The skirt was flared silk that fell just below my knees. The two-inch-heeled black sandals with rhinestone butterfly accents elevated my petite frame a little. I left my hair down, the black ringlets framing my face and shoulders. Because my lashes were so long and thick, I never used mascara, which shortened my makeup time. I only wore eyeliner, a hint of eye shadow, and lip gloss.

"Maybe I should go and grab my can of mace to fend off the ravenous teenage wolves."

"Angelo!" I laughed. "You're crazy!"

"We shall see."

"Well, you always look great." He was wearing a black suit with a deep blue dress shirt and a gray and blue silk paisley print tie. The blue shirt made the blue of his eyes even more vivid. I reached up and brushed the hair back from his forehead, softly touching the scar. I always did that. I knew Suzanne had always made him feel self-conscious of it and that was probably the reason he grew his hair out, but instead of the scar taking away from his attractiveness, it only added to it. Smiling up at him, I took his hand and we went to dinner.

That night, Cara sat next to Angelo again. The skin-tight, low-cut red dress she wore hardly left anything to the imagination. Shaylee's dress was almost identical. Glancing at Angelo, I could read the disapproval in his expression and my heart lightened. Finding a modest formal dress hadn't been easy, but I was glad I did. I watched Cara, keeping my expression blank. Angelo caught me staring and I quickly smiled at him and started talking with Shaylee about the fun afternoon we had. Shaylee joked with me about the attention I attracted from the guys at the club. She called me stuck up for not giving them the time of day, to which I responded, "I wasn't being snobby, I just have standards, and taste." Then we both laughed.

I watched Cara take a large gulp of her wine and scoot even closer to Angelo. She joked with him about his shuffleboard skills, placing a hand on his arm every now and then, and on his leg once, which made my insides clinch in anger. I suddenly wanted to slap her. I wanted to pull her hair from her roots. The violent thoughts were startling, and I quickly put myself in check.

Angelo looked uncomfortable and it was safe to say there would be no cruise ship matchup for him. Leaning toward me slightly, he draped an arm across the back of my chair, pressing a hand against my hair affectionately. I gave him a loving smile and continued bantering with Shaylee about the 'stalker boys' as we called them.

After dinner, we all went to the atrium to listen to a little live music until it was time for the comedy show. The early show was supposed to be family friendly and Angelo and I were looking forward to it. I could see there would be no need to invite Cara and Shaylee. They were inviting themselves.

There was a brother duo performing in the atrium. One was on the guitar, the other on the keyboard, and their vocals were great. They were performing a set of classic pop songs.

In the middle of the set, one of the brothers said, "Hey, we would like to invite a daring soul to come up and help us out with this next song. It's an old classic and one I'm sure most of us are familiar with. So, do we have any takers?"

The crowd stirred, but no one was moving toward the stage.

"Come on, I know there's someone with a great voice. Who wants to give it a try?"

I scanned the crowd again, wondering if anyone else would be daring enough to go up. Riding a moment of courage, I released Angelo's hand and moved toward the stage.

"Yes!" the singer said. "I knew there was

someone willing to help us out." He asked me my name and age and where I was from, then he said, "Are you ready for this, Katia?"

When I smiled and nodded, he said, "Okay, guys, we're going to do an Ike and Tina Turner tune. Katia, you know *Proud Mary*, right?"

"Yes, I do."

"All right, we've got the words here just in case you need them."

"I'm good," I said.

"Okay, guys, looks like we've got a little pro here. All right, Katia, we'll harmonize with ya, but this is all you, so strut your stuff, okay?"

"Okay."

Holding the mike, I looked out at Angelo's wide eyed stare and gave him a cheeky grin. To say he was surprised was an understatement. Then the music started and I began to sing. Proud Mary has always been one of my favorite songs. The brothers' voices were soon soaring with mine, the three of us blending in perfect harmony. All around the atrium, hands were clapping, bodies moving to the beat. I couldn't believe I was really on the stage doing this.

When we finished, the cheers and applause were thunderous, and the crowd begged for an encore. The two men praised me and asked me to sing another song. I agreed and whispered my song choice. They nodded and I took a seat behind the unoccupied piano. One of the singers moved a mike stand by me and adjusted the height until it was perfect. They searched their tablets and found the sheet music to accompany me. I knew the song by heart and needed no sheet music.

I performed the classical-pop ballad, *Broken Vow*. Closing my eyes, I lost myself in the music, only this time as I sang it, I was driven by a new emotion I couldn't quite define.

As I sang the final line, I opened my eyes, and again the hall rocked with applause. Both the men hugged me and thanked me for singing with them, and I received congratulating pats on the back as I moved through the crowd, making my way back to Angelo. I grinned as he swept me up in a big hug.

"Well, you are just full of surprises, aren't you, Katoosha? When did this new skill develop?"

Drawing his head down, I whispered, "I took some online lessons to perfect my singing voice. I figured I would surprise you one day."

He chuckled. "Well, you definitely picked a fine time to do that." I laughed. "You were wonderful. I'm so proud of you."

"Thank you."

Cara and Shaylee told me how much they enjoyed my performance. I thanked them and we made our way back up to the lounge, hoping there were still good seats available for the comedy show. "Amazing," Angelo kept murmuring as we walked. I just laughed, holding tightly to his hand.

The Change

The rest of the cruise went by quickly. We spent the next day on the island of Barbados at a beach called *The Boatyard*. Just fifteen dollars got us in and included a beach chair, umbrella, and a free cup of fruit juice. We started the morning going scuba diving with the sea turtles and videoed with Angelo's underwater camera. The rest of our time was spent swimming and relaxing on the beach under the umbrella. We brought books and read for a bit, then we fell asleep for a while, making us both grateful for the umbrella. Without it, we would have gone back to the ship blistered and miserable. When we woke, the beach was filling with fellow tourists from the ship and we were glad we'd gotten there early.

Natives walked along the beach, selling jewelry, and Angelo bought a turtle bracelet for me, and a necklace for Kate. We planned to leave soon, but for a short while, we did a little people-watching.

Many of the native men wore their hair in the signature dreads, most of them even longer than the women. The citizens of Barbados spoke English, but at times it sounded like a completely different language.

As we got up to pack up our things, a man approached us, trying to sell us aloe vera gel that he had extracted and squeezed into a pint-size rum bottle. Angelo politely told him we were not interested and he moved on to the next person, only to have a policeman escort him off the beach because he did not have a permit to sell there. As we were exiting, we spotted the man standing near the gate. I went to him and slipped him a five-dollar bill. He gave me a big toothy grin in return.

Draping an arm around me, Angelo said, "You just couldn't resist, could you?"

I smiled. "He was an enterprising man, which is better than doing nothing."

Shaking his head, he smiled and kissed my

cheek.

* * *

That night, there was a band playing Latin music. Having finished eating, I grinned widely at Angelo and he laughed, reading my mind. He grabbed my hand and we joined the couples dancing in front of the stage. I loved dancing with Angelo. He was a great dancer and his samba and salsa were amazing. I was aware of the envious stares of the women watching us and I allowed myself to really look at Angelo, glimpsing, not for the first time, what other women saw. He really was beautiful. He had no idea just how amazing he was.

The band ended the song and went right into a ballad.

"One more for the road," Angelo said. As he drew me close, my emotions started acting a little strange, and my heart felt a little weird all of a sudden. I wondered if I was coming down with something and figured I must have just been tired. I tended to feel a little off when I was tired.

No, that's not it at all, and you know it. Laying my head against his chest, I closed my eyes against the burning tears pressing. *Don't do this!* I mentally chastised myself. *Don't!*

* * *

When I got back to my room, I quickly readied myself for bed because we would be getting an early start the next morning. With a great deal of effort, I shut my brain and emotions off so that I could not ponder too deeply the feeling from earlier, and I managed to drift off.

* * *

In St. Kitts the following day, we took another bus tour. In St. Lucia and St. Martins, we did more sightseeing and shopping. I told Angelo it was a good thing we brought two large suitcases and packed light because it was the only way we would get everything home.

On the final night of the cruise, we order room service for dinner and watched my favorite movie, *Somewhere in Time* on Angelo's laptop in my room. It would be the first time Angelo had ever watched it. The story was about a playwright who sees a photograph of a beautiful woman hanging in the hotel where he is staying, and falls madly in love with her. Then through self-hypnosis, he travels back in time to be with her. I had always told Angelo how romantic it was, and since I loved it so much, he bought the movie for me before we came on the cruise. I saved it to watch on the ship.

The full day slowly caught up with me and it was hard to keep my eyes open. I was so tired, I fell asleep against Angelo's shoulder, and finally woke a little as he turned off the movie. I smiled at him as he tucked me into bed just like when I was little, kissed my brow, and whispered goodnight.

However, after he closed the door, I awakened fully. Sitting up, I rested my face in my hands and pondered the past two days and what was happening to me.

And when I finally let myself admit exactly what it was, I lay back down, pulled the covers over me, and cried myself to sleep.

* * *

The next morning, we left the ship and stood in line with our luggage, waiting to get through customs. Cara and her daughter were standing in another line and they waved. We waved back and inched forward as the line moved.

They caught us just as we'd exited and were about to cross the street. We were planning to leave our luggage at the hotel until we could check in. Unfortunately, they were staying at the same hotel. Angelo glanced at me and I quickly smiled. I was sure it didn't look sincere this time, but he gave me a look that said he understood. We only had two days in San Juan and the last thing I wanted was for them to intrude upon our time together.

After spending the morning with Cara and Shaylee tagging along with us everywhere–and Cara trying to attach herself to Angelo at every opportunity–we checked in and were heading up to our suite, when to my joyful surprise, Angelo finally told her that it had been fun getting to know her, but the rest of the time would be his and mine. While Shaylee and I took a moment to say goodbye to each other, Cara pulled a piece of paper from her purse, scribbled her contact info on it and handed it to Angelo.

"Call me some time," she said before brushing her lips against his cheek, and every nerve inside me pulsed, causing a deep ache. It was a sudden sense of loneliness, one that I had not felt in a long time. And I needed to find a way to handle it.

That night before going to bed, I told Angelo, "When we get home, I would like to get a drum set."

* * *

Each and every day after that trip, I buried my heart in my music, my dance, my art.

But all these things served to add layer upon layer of beautiful agony to an ache that I didn't think would ever go away.

Heartsick

Three years later

Sylvia and I had lunch, which we'd finished some time ago. I had invited her because I needed to talk. Now, she just sat and patiently waited while I quietly gathered my thoughts.

"He's going on a date tonight."

"Another date that you encouraged him to go on," Sylvia stated. "His sixth or seventh in three years if I'm remembering correctly."

I silently nodded, my insides twisting up in knots.

"You're not happy about him dating, are you? You never have been." When I said nothing, she asked, "What about you? When is the last time you went out with someone?"

"I can't remember."

"I do. It was six months ago. In in the past three years, you have dated even less than he has. Why is that?"

I needed to answer her. I desperately needed to confide in her and share what I had carried inside for three long years, but I had no clue how to even begin. And what would she think of me when I did speak the words–words that my heart had considered forbidden to utter for so long?

Sylvia's wise eyes stared into mine, and then I knew *she* knew.

"When did you begin to fall in love with him?"

With her earnest question, the floodgates of my mind opened and my thoughts slowly tumbled through my lips.

I loved Angelo De Luca more than words could possibly express. I couldn't really pinpoint when I knew for sure, but looking back, I realized my feelings for him began to change even before the cruise, they just didn't start to materialize until then.

Wiping away the tears that came unbidden, I remembered wondering if something was wrong with me. And even though I had tried to shake it off and go on pretending things were normal, I couldn't. For me, everything was changing then. *I* was changing, though it took me a while to realize just what was happening to me.

Many times during the cruise, I had caught myself staring at Angelo when he wasn't looking. Whenever we stood on the deck looking out over the ocean, I found myself watching the breeze tousle his dark hair, marveling at the vividness of his blue eyes and the way his tanned skin looked in the sun. I had felt an unfamiliar warmth curl in my stomach on the morning we docked in St. Martins when he opened the door to let me in before he'd even put his shirt on. The muscles of his arms and chest were lean and chiseled. I had seen him without a shirt plenty of times before, and had spent time swimming and on the beach with him shirtless. But that day I was seeing him in a different light. Angelo looked like an untouchable Italian god. He was so handsome–he always had been, but only then did I truly admit to myself that I was attracted to the man that raised me, the man who had cared for me for most of my life.

Each and every day after that trip, my feelings continued to grow until I couldn't deny it any longer. I deeply loved him. I may have been young, but my heart had known what it wanted. Over the years, that want had become a need, one that was so strong, I could barely conceal it, and I was scared to death of him finding out.

"I don't know what to do," I finally said. "He still sees me as a child and probably always will. One day he will find someone else. He will fall in love and marry again. And I don't know if I could handle that."

"Yes, he will marry again one day," Sylvia said. "And no, you wouldn't be able to handle that. But you won't have to."

"What do you mean?"

Sylvia looked at me intently. "Angelo doesn't think of you as a child anymore, Katia. He sees you as a woman, a very beautiful woman. I can't say what is going on inside his heart, but think about this. The only reason he dates–when he does date–is because you encourage him. If you didn't, I don't think he would go out at all. He would much rather be home with you."

I shook my head, unable to believe that. Angelo and I had always been close and I knew he loved me, but it was the love of a caretaker.

"Think about it Katia. Think long and hard about it."

I allowed myself to think about the few dates Angelo had gone on and how generic they were. Whenever he came home, I was waiting. I always had. The secret warmth I felt when he walked through the door was always mixed with an ache that grew more acute each time. I would immediately ask him how his date went. Our conversations always went the same way. I would ask, "How was your date?" He would answer, "It was all right." Next, I'd ask, "What did you do?" Then he would tell me. Usually it was dinner and a movie. I always tried to smile brightly, but it was not my real smile. It was my masking smile. There were secrets behind my smile he had yet to glimpse, and I would never let him discover what they were.

After he would tell me about his date, we would pop some popcorn and play a game or watch television, where I would fall asleep against his shoulder. During the past year, whenever this happened, I would wake up with his arm around me and his lips pressed against my brow, and the warmth spreading through me was instant. It took everything to keep from sighing audibly. During those moments, the want and emotional need were so tangible, I would end up crying myself to sleep.

As I thought back on the three dates I had over the past year, something occurred to me. Whenever I left, his eyes always held something I couldn't discern. They almost seemed sad. And when I returned, his reaction was the same as mine when I waited for him.

Could he . . .

Evidently Sylvia was a mind reader, because she placed her hand over mine and said, "It's time, Katia. It's time for you and Angelo." She smiled. "You are a woman now, and it is your time to love."

"But maybe he won't –"

"Katia, trust me. It is time. But first, you need some time on your own."

"What do you mean?"

"I have a condo in Nags Head. It's yours to use. Get away for a little while and sort it through."

As much as it would kill me to be away from Angelo, Sylvia was right. I did need some time. Maybe a couple of months away would be good for me. But what would Angelo think?

"So, should I have the on-call housekeeper get the condo ready for you?"

I couldn't think about it anymore or I would talk myself out of it. No matter how much it would hurt, I needed to do this.

"Yes," I finally answered. "I'll leave this weekend."

* * *

It was a little before midnight when I got home. Angelo was still up, most likely waiting for me and wondering why I wasn't there when he got back from his date. I felt bad about that. When I'd called him earlier, I only said I had a few more errands to run and I would see him later. I hadn't said how much later, and I felt guilty for not being there.

I met him in the upstairs hallway. We stood looking at each other, neither of us seeming to know what to say. I was afraid to say what I needed to say. Maybe tomorrow I would tell him, when I could think it over a little more.

After staring into his eyes a moment, I sensed a change, one that made my heart pound.

Why is he looking at me that way? I wondered. He finally spoke first.

"I talked to Sylvia."

"Oh." *So, that's why.* Closing my eyes, I turned away from him. I could feel myself trembling. Sylvia was supposed to let me tell him.

"I had called her earlier," he said.

287

"Because I . . . needed to talk."

I felt him slowly move closer. He gently took my shoulders in his hands, turning me around. He lifted my chin, urging me to look at him, and I fought back the tears pressing. He pressed his lips to my closed lids, and then my cheeks, gently kissing the tears away. At the touch of his warm mouth against my skin, I shuddered and exhaled. When he finally spoke again, his voice was rough with emotion, his blue eyes misty.

"Katia, *dolcezza*, I understand why you must leave. Take all the time you need. But know that I will be here waiting for you."

He drew me into his arms then, and I melted against him. His arms were so warm, his embrace more intoxicating than ever before. I could feel his heart pounding like mad and it matched the beat of my own. I moved my hands up his taunt, muscular back and held him tighter.

Neither of us spoke again. We simply stood there, locked in an emotional embrace. I never wanted him to let me go. I could stay wrapped in his arms this way forever.

The Separation

On the day of my departure, we were both an emotional wreck, and it was apparent that Sylvia had been right. I needed to go. As much as it would hurt, we really did need to learn how to be apart for a while.

Over the past few days, we shared our thoughts, feelings, fears, and hopes. Angelo had been nervous about embracing this change between us, but I did my best to soothe his inner concerns about him being enough for me. It hurt my heart that he would worry about that, and I hoped I helped him to truly see that he was more than enough. His age did not matter. The fact that he raised me did not matter. He was all I ever wanted and more, much more.

We talked, laughed, and were our usual selves, only nothing was the same. There was a new awareness of one another. We shared lingering looks and longing gazes. Angelo was such a beautiful man. He had always had been, but now that we were open to one another, I could truly appreciate his beauty and his attractiveness.

The sly grins that once charmed me now warmed and excited me, making me feel the things I had never felt before. Womanly things. Everything he did or said now affected me differently. Even holding hands and sitting together by the lake had a newness that awakened my senses and quickened my emotions. We did the same things we always did together, but now each activity was done with the knowledge that an unexpected future was before us.

And now I was leaving. I felt like I was literally leaving a part of myself behind.

Before we left for the airport, Angelo slipped something into my bag and told me not to open it until after I boarded the plane. I promised him I would wait.

Saying goodbye to Angelo at the security gate was the hardest thing I had ever done. We held each other tightly. He buried his face in my hair and I pressed mine against his chest, hiding my tears. I ached so much, I could barely breathe.

Finally drawing back, I looked up into his eyes and gently caressed his hair, burying my hand in its thick softness. "I'll miss you, Angelo."

"And I'll miss you." He caressed my face and I longed for him to kiss me, but I knew he would rather wait until I returned and we were alone. A few nights before, he explained to me that as much as he wanted to share a first kiss with me, he wanted to give me time. He wanted to court me, and I understood. While it may have been an old-fashioned notion to most, it was most romantic to me, and so Angelo.

He caressed my face, staring into my eyes. "Come back to me, *amore*. Please."

"I will. I promise." I kissed the corner of his mouth, lingering a moment. Then I turned and got in line.

I kept looking back, watching him watch me until I was past security and he was no longer in sight.

* * *

I kept my emotions in check until I boarded the plane and was settled in my seat. I was flying in first-class and so far, no one was sitting next to me. Unable to hold back any longer, I discreetly turned my face toward the window and let the tears come.

The last few days had been so amazing. Love washed over me, through me, as I thought about all we shared. Dinner and a show at the theater afterwards. A picnic lunch in the park. A fun-filled day at Universal Studios. Sitting by the lake in the dark, wrapped in his arms, looking up at the stars. We had done all those things before, but this time everything was new. Being in love had changed and intensified everything.

Drawing my thoughts to the present, I reached into my tote bag for a pack of tissues and my eyes fell on the small wrapped box and envelope Angelo put there. Drying my eyes, I opened the envelope and pulled out the small note card.

My Dearest Katia,

There are so many things I want to say to you. I hardly know where to start, but I will share with you the most important.

First and foremost is that I am in love with you, il tesora mia. *You truly are my treasure, my priceless treasure, and I love you with every breath I breathe. You have been a part of me for a very long time, and I long to make you a permanent part of me forever. But that is a question I will save until you are home again.*

Just know you are in my heart, amore, *and my arms will ache until you are in them again. It is your rightful place. It always has been.*

Yours always,

Angelo

Closing my eyes, I pressed the card to my heart, wanting to brand his words there. I had spent countless hours and moments dreaming of him saying those very words to me, but those dreams paled when compared to reality. During the past week, Angelo's words had been guarded, measured. Now he had said it. He loved me. After all this time of loving him silently, to have that love returned was everything. But I still needed time to adjust to this new change in our relationship, and so did he. I just hoped I would be able to survive the separation.

Placing the card back in my bag, I pulled out the box and unwrapped it, pressing a hand over my heart when I saw the actual ring box. I opened it, my vision immediately blurring as my eyes beheld the most beautiful ring I had ever seen. It was a one carat oval canary diamond surrounded by smaller stones and set on a diamond studded platinum band. Taking it from the box, I placed it on my finger. It was perfect, and the perfect ring for me. Angelo knew me well. By giving me the ring, he was making a pledge and a promise, as well as fully claiming me as his.

I was all right with that. Because he was all I had ever wanted.

Putting the box and the card back into my bag, I spotted the bottle of ibuprofen and fished it out, dumping a couple into my hand as the familiar pain that had come and gone over the past year grew more prominent. The back ache and stomach ache was usually manageable and I had never felt a need to worry.

But now I had a future with Angelo to look forward to. And that changed things.

Alone

I passed the days and weeks by taking daily walks along the beach, JKD workouts a couple of mornings a week, ballet on the hardwood dining room floor, and playing a rented violin and cello. Every now and then, pain forced me to sit those things out, but usually it wasn't for long.

Angelo and I talked every night, sometimes for hours. I loved the sound of his voice and I always asked him where he was in the house so I could picture him there. I missed him so much, and we stayed on the phone as long as possible. There were long moments when we didn't even speak, we just let ourselves *be* together, even though there were miles between us.

* * *

Sitting on the beach, I stared out at the ocean, listening to the roar of the rolling waves, and as usual, thought about Angelo. We had been apart for a month. I thought being away from him would get a little easier, but that was impossible, and I was glad, even though it hurt. I welcome that kind of pain.

But there was another kind of pain that I could no longer ignore. I had an appointment scheduled for the following day with a doctor Sylvia suggested. She had known the woman for years and they were good friends. When I called the day before, I made Sylvia promise that she wouldn't say anything to Angelo. It may not be anything serious and I didn't want him to worry. But to be truthful, though I was trying to remain positive, I was worried about what I would find out. What if the problem was something that affected us having children? How would Angelo take that kind of news? I knew he loved me and that it wouldn't change things between us, but it would still be disappointing not having a child of his own. Then again, we could always adopt.

Chastising myself for my negative thoughts, I attempted to clear my mind. It took some doing, but I managed.

However, as I knelt by my bed that night to pray, a voice whispered to my heart, "Be strong," and then and there, something inside me knew.

* * *

Almost two weeks later, my fears were confirmed, and the doctor's words left no room for denial. That night, I cried myself to sleep, my heart breaking for Angelo, and for me.

* * *

"How are you today?" Angelo asked me when I called him the next day.

I swallowed hard, not sure how to answer. "I'm okay."

"You don't sound okay. What's wrong, *dolcezza*?"

"I need to come home early. I'm flying in tonight. Can you meet me?"

"Of course, I can. But what is it?"

"I'll tell you when I come."

"You've got me worried, babe."

"I'm sorry, Angelo. It's not something I want to say over the phone. I really need to wait until I see you." I tried to disguise the emotion in my voice, but it wasn't working very well and I could hear the anxiousness in his.

"All right."

I told him my flight number and the arrival time.

"Angelo?"

"Yes?"

"I love you."

"I love you too. I will see you tonight."

* * *

When I passed through the security area and saw Angelo, I rushed through the crowd, flinging myself into his embrace. My body trembled as he held me close and I moved my arms from around his waist and circled his neck, clinging to him like a lifeline. His embrace tightened.

"I need you, Angelo," I whispered. "I love you and I need you."

"I am here, angel. I love you too, and I'm here."

Drawing back, I wiped my eyes. He took my hand and we went to get my luggage. He looked at the ring on my hand and smiled. I could sense his nervousness as we walked to the car, and before getting in, I hugged him again, pressing a lingering kiss to his cheek. I appreciated his patience more than I could say. Other than declaring how much we missed each other, the ride was mostly silent.

When we got home, Angelo took my luggage up to my room and I followed. We sat on the bed and he took my hands. "Please tell me, *tesorina*. What's wrong?"

Loosening one of my hands, I softly caressed his face, feeling the soft stubble. I missed doing that. Instead of answering right away, I unzipped my suitcase and removed a large yellow medical envelope I watched Angelo press a hand over his heart, his eyes moving back to mine.

"I've been having irregular periods for a while."

"How long is a while?"

I hesitated. "For a year now."

I could see the thoughts churning in his head.

"You could have told me, Katia. You can tell me anything."

"I know, and I would have, but I read that sometimes it's normal. Sometimes there has also been a little pain in my stomach and back. I read that could be normal too."

"And sometimes it isn't," he said gently. "Did the doctor say you can't have children?"

I looked down for a moment. When I

raised my eyes to his, tears filled them and poured down my cheeks. "No."

* * *

Four little words.

"Stage four ovarian cancer."

Those four words changed everything. And they knocked the wind out of Angelo.

He pulled me to him and I felt him trembling. He said nothing. I didn't think he could, so I talked.

I told him I had already been through the tests and was scheduled to go through another round the next day.

When he could finally speak, his words were few.

"Oh, my Katia," he whispered brokenly over and over. "Oh, Katia."

* * *

Again, the tests were conclusive.

The doctor said it was rare for a woman my age to have ovarian cancer, and because it had been growing in my body for so long, it was out of control. The cancer had spread from my ovaries to my liver and the lymph nodes in my neck and breasts.

Sitting in the doctor's office, we digested the prognosis. Then we had a choice to make: I could have surgery and treatments, granting me an extra month at the most, or enjoy the quality of life I had while I could. Drawing forth courage I didn't know I had, I made my choice, accepting the fact that either way, the cancer would end my life. So. I chose to live my life and enjoy all the time I had left with Angelo. I would take supplements and continue to exercise for as long as I could, and when the pain worsened, I would manage it with prescription medication. Neither of us could think past that.

That evening, Angelo told me he needed to be alone and I let him go. Sitting in his favorite chair, I waited for him to come back.

When he returned, his red eyes were the evidence of a good long cry. He told me he went for a drive out to Coco Beach and walked the beach for a while. He had been angry with God. After calming down, he had apologized to God for getting angry. He said I was God's before I was his and he had no right to be angry.

That night, we lay in Angelo's bed, holding one another and crying for the shortened life we would have together as man and wife. I couldn't stand the thought of leaving him alone and my heart broke to think of the separation. He didn't know how he would go on without me.

We had only just discovered our love, and now he would have to face losing me. We cried for the children we'd secretly dreamed of, children that would never be ours. Children that would have had their father's eyes, his smile. They would be so beautiful. Leaving him alone without a part of me to love was a hard thing to face, and I never knew I could hurt so much.

It was during this sharing of pain and sorrow that Angelo finally kissed me for the first time. The kiss started out slow and tender, as a first kiss should be. But soon, raw and desperate emotion seeped into the kiss, and a burning rolled through me, spreading over my entire body as the heat of his mouth and the scent and taste of him filled my senses. I had never been kissed before and this was all new to me. I was inexperienced in matters of intimacy and desire, but desire and passion are what I felt. The feel of his hands in my hair and on my body invoked a level of want and need that I had never imagined. I couldn't have imagined it if I tried. Being in his arms was heaven. We became lost in each other and restraint was slipping.

Exercising every bit of self-control he could muster, Angelo parted his mouth from mine and just held me against his heart. Then we fell asleep.

The following day, we dried our tears and drew courage to the surface, determined to face everything head-on and enjoy all the time we had left together, which meant marrying as soon as possible. And with Sylvia and Kate's help, we pulled the wedding together quickly.

When the three had agreed to our request to come over that morning and we broke the news of my health, Kate had excused herself and left the room for a moment, while Sylvia and Lee wept openly. When Kate returned with reddened eyes, she smiled, hugged us both and said, "Enough of that. We've got a wedding to plan." Her blanket statement had provided us all with a good chuckle.

That week we created the invitations and got them printed, and planned the reception. We bought my gown and Angelo's tux, as well as a tux for Lee, dresses for Sylvia and Kate, both of whom would be my maids of honor, and dresses for my bridesmaids.

When Angelo and I called Kimberly, Alison, and Denise and told them of our plans to marry, and I asked them to be my bridesmaids, each was a little subdued. But it didn't take them long to warm to the idea of us marrying, and they were excited and supportive. They had been a part of my life for years and knew us well. All three said yes to my request.

Angelo planned the honeymoon and said it was a surprise. It didn't matter to me where we went, I just wanted to be with him.

We spent many days by the lake, holding each other. We didn't talk much, but we really didn't need to. Just the physical contact was enough.

The night before the wedding, as we watched the stars slowly appear in the darkening sky, Angelo said, "I need to tell you something, Katia."

"Okay." I drew back a little and looked into his eyes. His handsome face was shadowed, the distant light from the pathway lamppost allowing me to just make out his features.

"When I married Suzanne, I did love her, and I was sure we were meant to be together. But soon after we were married, the real Suzanne showed her true colors and I knew I'd made a mistake. I was determined to keep trying and had hoped she would change. I thought that when we got you, it would prompt her to change." He paused, gazing out over the lake. "I finally realized that she had to want to change, and she didn't want it enough. But going through all of it led me to you."

I caressed his face and he kissed my palm.

"I may have loved Suzanne, but when I compare it to what I feel for you, there is no comparison, because loving you makes me feel alive, *tesora.* You make me truly feel alive in so many ways. I ache to have you as my wife and share that love in every way."

His words of love and devotion brought tears to my eyes and left me speechless. So, I pressed my lips to his and let my heart do the talking.

Solemn Vows

I felt so beautiful in my white gown. The silk, lace and tulle were accented by winking crystals on embroidered roses and flowed over my petite figure. My hair was piled high on my head, held in place with a crystal-beaded comb (a gift from Angelo) and a few curly locks framed my face. I wore no veil. I felt like a princess. Angelo said I *was* a princess to him. His tuxedo consisted of black slacks and a white jacket with a red bow tie and vest. I picked it out and he was happy to let me. He said all that was important was I would soon be his.

My arm was wrapped around Lee's as we walked toward the vine-covered Italian gazebo in our back yard, where I would bind myself to

Angelo. All one-hundred-fifty chairs were filled and we were awed by the support we'd received. No one had judged us when we announced that we were getting married, with the exception of one person. The negativity was from a long-time neighbor who told Angelo how wrong it was to marry me and how much he disgusted her for taking advantage of me that way. She definitely was *not* at the wedding, which suited us fine.

Kimberly, Alison and Denise looked beautiful in their yellow bridesmaid gowns, and I was so grateful to have them there.

Sylvia, Kate, and Lee looked wonderful in their wedding attire as well. (Sylvia and Kate were my maids of honor.) They were the only people who knew about my condition, and all three had tears trailing down their faces before the reverend began to speak. Words could never express how much I treasured their friendship.

When I reached Angelo, he took my hand in his, never taking his eyes from mine. As we gazed at one another, I felt as if we could see into each other's soul. With a great deal of effort, we finally turned, giving our attention to Reverend Sandler and he began.

"We are gathered here today in the sight of God to join Angelo and Ekaterina together in holy matrimony. As I stand here watching them together, I feel their love radiating around us, and I know that no two people were more meant for each other."

He gave us a kindly smile, his eyes misty. "Now, Angelo and Ekaterina have written their own vows."

The reverend gestured for Angelo to go first. Facing me, he held my hand against his chest and I felt his steady heartbeat.

"Katia, there are no words to describe what you mean to me. No words are good enough. You have brought such joy and happiness into my life. I love you so much, my heart cannot hold it all. You are the air I that breathe. I promise to love, honor and cherish you, and always be faithful to you, through the good times and the bad. My love for you is unconditional, Katia, and I promise you that my love will see you through clear skies and stormy days. No matter what comes . . . I will love you through it, forever and beyond." I watched him swallow hard, the tears falling down his face matching my own. He reached out and gently wiped mine away. There was so much love in his eyes, his very gaze branded me. His name was written upon my heart. It always had been.

The reverend prompted me to speak my vows.

"Angelo, you have been everything to me for as long as I can remember. You have cared for me, sheltered me, and loved me. When I thought I had no one, you were there." I paused as a river of fresh tears came. "And I know you always will be. I love you with all that I am. I promise to love, honor and cherish you, and always be faithful to you, through the good times and the bad. My love for you is unconditional, Angelo, and I promise you that my love will see you through clear skies and stormy days. No matter what comes, I will love you through it, forever and beyond."

Wiping his eyes, Reverend Sandler continued.

"Angelo, do you accept Ekaterina as your lawfully-wedded wife?"

"I do," he answered firmly.

"Ekaterina, do you accept Angelo as your lawfully-wedded husband?"

"I do," I replied with equal firmness.

We then exchanged rings and the reverend said, "By the power vested in me I pronounce you, Angelo and Ekaterina, husband and wife."

Taking me in his arms, Angelo whispered,

"I love you." I whispered that I loved him too, and, holding tightly to each other, we shared our first kiss and man and wife. I would forever remember this as the happiest moment of my life.

We quickly moved over to the reception area and stood in front of an iron, floral-draped arbor where we were congratulated, hugged and wished well.

The band was playing one of our favorite songs as Angelo led me up to the large, square platform for a dance. Even though there were couples swaying around us, we were lost in our own little world. I gazed around for a moment, taking in every beautiful detail before returning my eyes to his.

"Happy?" I asked.

I smiled, so completely in love. "Extremely."

"So am I."

"Thank you, Angelo. This is the best wedding day I could have asked for. Everything is perfect."

"You are perfect," he said, kissing me. Closing my eyes, I rested my brow against his chin as he held me closer. We danced through another song before heading to the bride and groom table to eat.

The food was catered by the hotel restaurant and was perfect as always. Ours was a traditional Italian wedding dinner and there were twelve courses, starting with antipasto appetizers and ending with a beautiful Italian wedding cake, made to my specifications. There were plenty of food choices to satisfy everyone. Neither of us wanted alcohol served at our wedding, and the guests seemed content with the flowing sparkling cider.

We were toasted throughout the meal, receiving various wishes for a happy marriage, long life, and many children. Angelo and I simply smiled at one another, words of love and encouragement silently spoken through our mutual gazes. Though we were saddened by the fact that some of the wishes were not possible, we wouldn't dwell on those things. This was our day. Our hearts were wrapped in love and we were warmed by the knowledge that we would be together forever.

When we finally left our guests and went into the house to change for our trip, Angelo told me we were going to Mackinac Island for our honeymoon. My favorite movie was still *Somewhere in Time* and I was ecstatic about spending our honeymoon in the place it was filmed. Angelo said it was only because there was a cancellation that we were able to get into the *Grand Hotel.* Most reservations were done far in advance at this time of year. We were fortunate enough to even get a suite.

My things were now moved in with Angelo's, but we decided to change in separate rooms, which only increased our anticipation of finally giving ourselves to one another. Angelo put our luggage in the trunk, and we drove off an hour later amid cheers and farewells and headed to the airport.

Mackinac

We flew into Pellston City, Michigan and took a taxi to the lodge where we had reservations for the night. The hotel was just minutes away from Mackinac City where we would then take the ferry over to Mackinac Island. I was beyond excited, and Angelo chuckled joyously at my giddiness. Our room at the lodge was nice and cozy, and I was looking forward to spending our wedding night there.

Kissing Angelo's lips lightly, I went into the bathroom with my overnight bag, closing the door behind me. Glimpsing my reflection in the mirror, I stood for a moment, holding my hands against my flushed cheeks. The cause of this rush of heat wasn't nervousness, but anticipation and desire. I was coming to him completely inexperienced, and I was grateful to have the gift of sexual purity to give him. I was also grateful for his experience. I said a silent prayer that none of the pain from my illness would intrude upon our night. I had sensed Angelo's nervousness, but I knew he would be tender with me. He would be the first and only man I ever made love with, and I wanted to remember every single moment.

Pulling the comb from my hair and giving my curls a shake, I quickly changed into the gown I had purchased for tonight and exited the bathroom. Angelo had turned down the bed and was sitting on the edge. He stood as I approach him. He was shirtless and beautiful. His hands shook as he drew me to him, but as soon as I wrapped my arms around him and pressed myself against his muscular body, I was lost. Our kiss was full of passion, the taste of one another stoking the fire burning between us, each touch creating a mutual hunger and thirst that were only assuaged when we finally became one.

* * *

"I never knew it would be like that," I said, resting my head against his chest, looking up at him with a loving smile. "I've dreamed about it almost every day since putting your engagement ring on my finger, but . . . I never realized." Truthfully, no imagining could have ever prepared me for the love I had just experienced with him.

Caressing my face, he kissed me, whispering against my lips, "It was never like this for me before."

Surprised, I drew back a little, looking into his eyes, wonder filling mine. "Never?"

He shook his head with an earnest smile. "Never."

Not even with Suzanne? My trembling lips curved. "I'm so grateful to have experience it, with you." Words failed me and I couldn't say more. But in his eyes, I saw understanding. One day this part of our marriage would no longer be possible. I knew he would miss it, but I also knew his love for me was strong enough that we would be okay.

He caressed my back. "I am grateful as well. We must savor the experience while we can." Smiling, he kissed me again, whispering, "I plan to take advantage of every opportunity to make love to you."

I grinned. "You took the words right out of my mouth, Mr. De Luca. So how about you take advantage of another opportunity now?"

"Mrs. De Luca," he murmured, rising over me, "you don't have to ask me twice."

* * *

Later, I fell asleep in his arms, listening to his heartbeat. I had never felt so fulfilled, or so happy.

* * *

The next morning, we had breakfast and checked out, anxious to be on our way. Taking a taxi to the dock, we boarded the ferry with our luggage.

Once we were settled in our seats, we took a few selfie shots with Angelo's camera. He kept his arm around me and I relished the wind on my face as we sailed to Mackinac Island. I pointed excitedly to the Round Island Lighthouse in the distance, which was used for one of my favorite scenes in the movie.

The *Grand Hotel* soon stood before us in the distance like a beacon and my heart began to pump faster. This was a dream come true for me. Photos and movie shots were one thing, but actually seeing the grand building was indescribable. The stunning hotel was well over a century old, a beautiful historical treasure.

When we reached the island dock, we

grabbed our luggage and took a horse-drawn taxi to the hotel. Surreal was the only word I could use to describe the experience of riding up the main road to the hotel. I was so excited to see the famous *Grand Hotel* sign, I squealed and hugged Angelo tightly. He laughed, holding me close.

We entered the lobby and Angelo chuckled as I released a dreamy sigh. Most of the decor was authentic and I could picture the lobby scene from the movie. I stood gazing around while he checked us in, imagining Christopher Reeve's character checking in the first time before going *back* in time. Then we went up to our room, taking in everything along the way.

I released another romantic sigh when we walked into the suite, and so did Angelo. It was one of the most beautiful rooms I had ever seen. Completely decorated in an eclectic mix of nineteenth century decor and a color scheme of pastels and floral patterns, it was a Victorian lover's dream room.

The bellboy placed our luggage in the room and Angelo tipped him. He thanked us and left.

Angelo had ordered an anniversary welcome package and a honeymoon basket for us. They sat on the table. I loved him for wanting everything to be perfect for me.

I walked around the room, running my hand over the black, gold-trimmed desk and allowing my fingers to skim over the matching foot-board of the bed. As the sudden need of his touch rolled through me, I turned to Angelo and smiled, meeting the look of mutual yearning and desire in his eyes, and we knew the unpacking would wait. He opened his arms and I moved into his embrace.

* * *

It was a little after noon when we finally made it down for the Grand Luncheon Buffet. The formal dining room overlooked the world's longest front porch–660 feet–lined with American flags. We were seated by the window, giving us a beautiful view of the Straits of Mackinac. The buffet was a sight to behold with a large variety of food. I was in heaven!

Angelo chuckled, watching me enjoy the delicious meal. He had brought his camera and was recording everything, wanting to capture every moment, and I understood why. If the situation had been reversed, I would have wanted to as well.

After lunch, we toured the inside of the hotel for a bit, taking a moment to look at the displays of items and props from the movie. I stopped for a long moment and gazed at the famous portrait of Elise that had Richard transfixed. Angelo told me he read that Christopher Reeve did not even see the picture until the actual filming so when he did finally see it, it would be a legitimate reaction. His expression of awe in the movie looked genuine to me, so it was a pretty smart idea. We browsed another moment before heading out to see one of the top places on my list: the "Is It You?" tree, where Richard and Elise met for the first time.

We walked down the boardwalk past the pool house and through the trees. The tree was located along the water's edge.

"This is amazing!" I said, standing next to the tree, reverently running my fingers over the bark. I read the plaque affixed to a stone.

"IS IT YOU?"
AT THIS SITE ON JUNE 27, 1912
RICHARD COLLIER FOUND ELISE
McKENNA

We asked another tourist who had just arrived to take our picture, and we imitated Richard and Elise's first meeting. My heart practically burst with love for Angelo, and the adoration in his eyes was priceless. We thanked the man and moved away so he and his wife could enjoy the site.

"That was perfect!" I said, hugging my handsome husband's waist. We stopped for a moment and he held me close, pressing a soft kiss to my lips.

"I'm glad." Kissing me again, he sighed dramatically and I laughed. "So where to next, *bella*?"

"What about taking a carriage into town for a bit? Could we?"

"Definitely."

* * *

Walking through town was like we had stepped back in time. We stopped by Baxter's Coin Shop for movie souvenirs, then we went to the theater where Elise declared her love for Richard during a play she was starring in. There was even a little plaque on the chair Richard sat in and I got a picture of Angelo kneeling next to the seat.

We stopped in the fudge shop and watched a fudge-making demonstration. Angelo and I both loved fudge and he bought a slice for us to share.

By now, I was getting tired. It saddened me how much my energy level had dipped.

Angelo noticed and took me back to the hotel.

When we got back, we took our purchases to our room and changed for dinner. I loved dressing up and had even purchased a few Victorian blouses online to wear. The one I chose to wear to dinner was ivory embroidered lace with long, slightly-puffed sleeves, a drawstring waist, and a high ruffled neck with a cameo. I paired it with a cream-colored slightly-flared skirt. Angelo told me I looked fabulous. He wore the beige Armani suit I picked out, wanting us to blend together. Though he had never worn a suit so light, he did for me, and he looked amazing.

After a light dinner, we decided to stop by the Terrace Room for a dance. We swayed to a ballad played by the hotel orchestra, then we sat at a corner table and listened for a while, watching a few couples swing dance. I grinned at Angelo, and soon we were up swinging right along with them. Dancing with Angelo was one of my favorite things to do.

By the time we made it back to our suite, I was exhausted and knew I had overdone it. I was experiencing a little pain, but I kept smiling, not wanting Angelo to worry. He grabbed some ibuprofen for me and I quickly took them. It had been a fun day, but I knew he would want me to take it easier during the rest of our time there.

"Tomorrow, we will take it a little easier," he said as we got into bed.

"I knew you would say that."

He quietly looked into my eyes. I continued to smile, but I knew he could see the pain creasing my brow. Touching my face, he gently drew me close, and I saw the tears in his eyes before he turned off the lamp.

"I'm sorry, *amore*."

"Shhh," I whispered, burying my fingers in his hair and drawing his head down, meeting his lips with mine in the dark. "I'll be fine," I whispered. "Don't worry. Will you just kiss me?"

Resting his head against mine for a moment, he whispered, "I love you," then did as I asked.

Preparing Angelo

We spent part of the next morning walking around the grounds, looking at the beautiful gardens and landscaping.

After lunch, we took a leisurely bike ride to see some of the sites around the island. I was experiencing some pain, but I managed it with Tylenol and ibuprofen.

We stopped to see Fort Mackinac, then we went to the butterfly conservatory. It was an all glass conservatory with lush plants surrounded by hundreds of butterflies in special greenhouses. Soft music played in the background.

"This is so awesome!" I said, lacing my fingers through Angelo's as we sat and watched all the different colors and breeds of butterflies.

"It is pretty amazing."

I sighed, taking in the glass sections surrounding us as various thoughts filled my mind. "You know, I read a book about a woman who had a near-death experience, and she said that in heaven the colors are even more vivid and beautiful than they are here. I'll bet the butterflies there are brilliant looking."

"I am sure you are right, *amore*," was all he said, but he didn't need to say anything else for me to know what was in his heart.

I turned and smiled lovingly, caressing his face, wishing I could smooth away the subtle sadness in his handsome features. He kissed my hand, holding it against his heart, and we took another moment to look before getting up to leave.

* * *

That evening after we had dinner, we went back up to our room and watched *Somewhere in Time*. I told Angelo before we came that since we were there, it was only fitting. This time he had a video cable, so we hooked his laptop up to the television and watched it.

This time, however, it was a little harder to watch. When Richard and Elise became separated by time and Richard ended up dying from a broken heart because he couldn't get back to her, the tears came in a rush, and though Angelo said nothing, I felt emotion rolling through him, could feel the pounding of his heart against my palm, hear it in my ear as I lay my head against his chest. His embrace tightened and his lips grazed my brow.

After a moment, I sat up and smiled. "Tomorrow we'll go and see the gazebo and stables, okay?"

Caressing my cheek, he smiled back and said, "Okay."

Accepting the Inevitable

It was our last morning in Mackinac when the pain began to worsen. We had just awakened when I sat up, releasing a low groan and taking a few deep breaths, the pain hitting me harder than normal.

Angelo kissed my brow. "Sweetheart, the Tylenol and ibuprofen are not going to work anymore."

I looked at him sadly. "I know." The worsening pain had been inevitable. He wiped my tears away, attempting to keep his own emotions at bay. "Will you get me my meds?"

Kissing my cheek, he into went to the bathroom and I was grateful we had gotten the prescriptions filled. In place of the over-the-counter medicine, I would now take morphine, a low dose antidepressant, and another medication to control the nausea. I had put it off for as long as I could. Now there was no choice. I had to take the stronger meds. The doctor told us he had been amazed that I'd stayed healthy for as long as I had. He attributed it to regular exercise and a good diet. That may have been true, but I was pretty certain God had something to do with it as well, and I would never stop thanking Him that Angelo and I realized our love for each other before it was too late.

He returned with a glass of water, the meds and supplements. He dumped the pills into my hand and I took them all at once. I lay my head against my loving husband's shoulder and he held me gently, trying not to hurt me. He would never want to cause me additional pain. He reached for the bakery box on the nightstand and gave me the last sweet roll to eat since I was supposed to take the medicines with food.

I took two small bites and chewed slowly. "I'm sorry, *amore*," I said, touching my face. "As soon as the meds kick in I'll shower and dress and we can go."

"You have nothing to be sorry for. We can do whatever you want. I just don't want you to overdo it, all right?"

"I won't, but I don't want to spend our final day stuck in the room. Even if we just go out for a little while, I'll be happy."

"Just promise me you will let me know when you need to come back."

"I promise."

There was so much sadness and pain in his blue eyes, but I knew he wanted to be strong for me. I was determined to enjoy our final day in Mackinac and he would help me do that. Drawing back a little, I looked up at him, and he smiled, kissing my lips. I gave him a brave smile in return, disguising the sadness I also felt.

"I think I can go and shower now."

"Okay, and while you are showering I'll order up some breakfast. Hopefully it will be here by the time you're done."

"Okay." Standing, I leaned down to kiss him. "*Ti amo*, Angelo," I whispered against his lips.

"I love you, too, *dolcezza*."

I managed to shampoo my hair and tame it into a loose bun, feeling no desire to attempt anything else. I dressed in one of the new outfits I'd bought the day before, wanting to look nice for Angelo. Of course, he always thought I was beautiful no matter what I wore.

When I came from the bathroom, Angelo had everything ready and we sat down at the table to eat. I looked at him a long moment, not missing the fact that he'd been crying. He smiled and I smiled back, tears filling my tired eyes. The medication was affecting me already. I suggested that we go sit out on the porch for a while and people-watch and Angelo grinned and said, "Whatever you want, *tesora mia*."

* * *

Taking a seat in the row of white rockers on the porch, we did sit and people-watch for a while. The view of the sea from where we sat was incredible. We held hands and silently enjoyed the soft morning sounds.

Yawning, I said, "I think we need to get up before I fall asleep."

"All right," Angelo said, standing and helping me up. "Let's go and browse the gift shop once more."

In the little shop, Angelo purchase a *Grand Hotel* music box for me. It was a replica of the one Elise owned in the movie, and when you opened the lid it played the beautiful Rachmaninoff theme from the movie. I in turn bought him a replica of the pocket watch Elise gave to Richard.

On the face was a picture of the two lead characters.

"Thank you for this," I said, kissing him. I hugged the package containing the music box, so excited to have it. "Thank you for an amazing honeymoon." I gave him a loving smile. "I feel like Elise and you're my Richard."

"Thank you for the watch, and for marrying me." He pressed a hand to my cheek. "And I doubt Richard could love Elise any more than I love you."

I wrapped an arm around his waist and we stood holding one another. I wished so much that I could find the words to tell him exactly what he meant to me.

We went back to our room and I lay down to rest for a while. Angelo curled himself around me, drawing my body protectively against his and napped with me. Later, when we awakened, we ordered dinner in and began to pack. By the time our meal arrived, I needed to take more pain medication. After we ate, we undressed and got into bed, deciding to leave the rest of the packing until the morning. Angelo held me for a while and we talked.

He lightly ran his fingers across the scar on my arm from the burn I'd gotten as a child.

"I probably should have had something done to it," I said, raising my eyes to his.

"I'm glad you didn't." He raised my arm to his lips and kissed the scar. "It is a part of you and I wouldn't want you to change it."

I smiled. "I can still remember the day a little. I vaguely remember getting the burn, but I do clearly remember trying to wake my mother up. Then you were there . . . and you made everything better. You always made everything better."

Angelo was quiet, lost in thought, and I could almost see what he was thinking. He and Suzanne had been arguing that day before coming for me. Years later, he told me why.

My eyes began to burn, my vision of his face blurring. "I'm so sorry that I can't give you a child, Angelo –"

"Don't be sorry," he said, brushing his lips over my temple. "You are enough."

"But when I'm gone –"

"I will have my memories of you. And I will look forward to the day when we can be together again."

"We *will* be together again."

Swallowing hard, he softly said, "We will."

Promises and Vows

I slept through much of the plane ride home, waking every now and then to find him looking at me intently. The deep love in his eyes reached into my heart, overwhelming me and making me want to weep. I returned his gaze for as long as I could before drifting off to sleep again.

On our way to the house, Angelo stopped by the hotel restaurant. Too tired to go in with him, I waited in the car while he ordered some of my favorite soup and sandwiches to go. When we made it home, I went up and changed into my gown while he brought everything inside. I came down and we ate the meal, then we unpacked and put things away.

Removing the music box from its packaging, he set it on my bedside table so I could always see it when I awakened each morning. I finally took my medication and lay back against the pillows, watching him put the last few things away. He opened the music box and I smiled, melancholy filling me as the Rhapsody gently played.

Angelo sat down on the bed beside me. "Can I get you anything?" He brushed the hair away from my face, tucking a small lock behind my ear. Unable to help it, tears filled my eyes and quickly spilled down my cheeks as a profound sadness swept over me. "What is it?"

"I'm just so sorry to put you through this."

"Oh, angel, don't be sorry. I love you. You are my wife and this is my place." As soft sobs burst from me, he crawled over next to me and drew me into his arms, pressing his lips to my brow, rocking me slowly.

"Don't cry, baby. Please don't feel sorry." I felt his tears drop into my hair. He finally drew back a little. "Look at me, Katoosha," he said and I raised my eyes to his. "Do you remember our wedding vows? We promised each other, Katia. I promised you we would get through this together." Holding me close, he softly recited our vows.

"*I promise to love, honor and cherish you, and always be faithful to you, through the good times and the bad. My love for you is unconditional, Katia, and I promise you that my love will see you through clear skies and stormy days. No matter what comes, I will love you through it, forever and beyond.*"

"That will never change, *tesora*." Holding me closer still, he said, "If there is one thing I have learned from the story of Richard and Elise, it is that true love transcends all things. Regardless of the circumstances, there is always hope." His voice cracked. "And though I will lose you for a time, I have hope, and the faith that we will be together again. I *know* we will. It is that knowledge that will keep me going on."

I touched his cheek. "I love you," I whispered, raising my mouth to his, letting the passion of his kiss roll through me. For as long as I could, I wanted to give him all I could. Because one day soon, I would have nothing left to give, only longing looks and the knowledge that my heart would be his for eternity.

* * *

Before leaving for work the next morning, Angelo placed my meds and a croissant and some juice on my bedside table. He talked with me for a few moments and reluctantly kissed me goodbye.

Feeling the pain slowly coming on, I took the medication with the juice, ate half the croissant, and lay in bed until the pain began to relent. At nine, I called Kate and asked her if she had time to come and cut my hair, hoping I'd caught her at a time that she wasn't suffering from morning sickness. Kate and Lee had called us the night before to welcome us home and share their news. Kate was finally pregnant again after years of trying. We were happy for them and would not allow sadness over our own inability to have a child diminish our joy.

Kate assured me that she was fine this morning and always had time for me. She came right over.

* * *

"What do you think?" Kate asked, handing me a mirror when she was done. She had given me a very short, tapered pixie cut.

My eyes moved over the thick tresses covering the floor a moment before gazing at my reflection. "I love it. Do you think Angelo will like it?"

"He will love it," Kate assured me. "Honey, you could have the worst haircut in the world and that man would still think you were the *most beautiful woman* in the world."

I smiled. "I still can't believe how much he loves me."

Kate grabbed the broom and started sweeping up the hair. "Angelo's heart was always meant to be yours, Katia."

How thankful I was for that. Blinking tears away, I nodded, brushing a hand over my short hair. "Thank you, Kate."

"You're welcome." She tied a small ribbon around a thick lock of the hair and handed it to me. "Keep it for Angelo."

Giving Kate a watery smile, I accepted the hair. I would place it in a small keepsake box I had brought back from our honeymoon.

After Kate left, I took a quick shower and dressed in a bohemian style skirt and a light, sleeveless crocheted blouse that I'd bought on Mackinac Island, wanting to look nice for Angelo. Then, putting together a list, I ordered groceries and had them delivered. As soon as I put everything away, I threw together a meatloaf and put it in the oven along with a couple of baked potatoes and set the timer.

By the time I finished, I was so tired, I lay down on the couch in the family room and covered myself with a light blanket, immediately falling asleep.

* * *

I awakened to the sound of the kitchen door opening. "Hi," I said sleepily, sitting up on the family room couch.

Placing his laptop and what looked like my favorite cake on the counter, Angelo came in and sat down, immediately taking me in his arms. He touched my hair, warming me with his adoring gaze.

"Do you like it?" I asked.

"I love it. You're beautiful."

"Thank you."

"How are you, *amore?*"

"I'm okay, just glad to see you."

Pressing a kiss to my lips, he murmured, "I'm glad to be home again. Now that I'm with you, all is right with the world."

I grinned and he kissed me again, and I let my hands get lost in his hair. I pressed myself against him and his embrace tightened gently. Heat, desire and need rolled through me, slowly rising in intensity.

"Angelo," I whispered, parting my mouth from his and looking into his eyes. The desire I saw in them mirrored mine.

"Are you sure?"

I nodded, a coy smile curving my lips.

"What about dinner?"

"It can wait." I drew his head down, claiming his kiss again, then moved my mouth over his jaw. As my lips lightly glided to his neck, he groaned.

"*Si, bella*. It can."

* * *

The pain that seized me in the middle of the night was intense and I gasped, curling myself into a ball.

"Katia?" came Angelo's voice, but I couldn't answer him. He turned on the lamp and rubbed my back. "Baby, I'll get your meds."

I groaned. It hadn't been that long since I took the last dosage. The doctor had instructed me to increase the amount, but I'd tried to hold off on doing that. It seemed now I would have no choice.

When Angelo returned, I slowly sat up, unable to stop the tears. His eyes filled as he handed me the pills and I took them. He urged me to lie back down with my back to him and he gently rubbed my back, pressing a kiss against my shoulder. His touch was soothing, and combined with the meds, the pain slowly began to relent. He said nothing, he just continued his gentle ministrations. But what he did not say carried a loud echo.

"Talk to me, Angelo," I softly prompted. "Tell me what you're thinking."

I heard him sniffle, and it was a full minute before he answered.

"I don't want to be without you." His voice was a broken whisper. "I want to go with you, to be wherever you are."

I turned over and held his face between my hands. His eyes were tightly shut, tears trailing over the bridge of his nose.

"Look at me, *amore mio*." When he finally opened his eyes, the anguish in them was almost more than I could bear. "You have to carry on for the both of us. As long as you live, I live. And we will be together again in God's time, not ours. Promise me you will never give up." I drew his head forward, pressing my mouth to his. "Promise me, Angelo," I whispered against his lips "Promise me. If for nothing else, promise me because you love me."

"I promise," he finally said, burying his face against my neck. "For you, I won't give up. Because I love you. I love you so much."

Breathing for Katia

Angelo

Katia stopped writing in her book of memories two weeks ago, her failing health making it impossible to continue. She slipped away peacefully in my arms today as I held her by the lake, and part of me left this world with her.

It is nighttime now; the visitors have gone, the house is barren, and I am alone in our bed, writing by lamplight, clinging to Katia's pillow and soaking it with my tears. I breathe deeply, inhaling her essence, then I breathe out and repeat. In and out. In and out. For a few precious moments, I feel her near, then she is gone. But I know she will be back, and I will live for that next moment, and the next.

Her body is gone, but only her body. And though we will be parted for a time, she left her words to bring me comfort, and the memories of our life together will help me to go on. Her spirit will live on, and so will her love.

She will forever be my treasure, and my heart will forever be hers.

About the Author

Jewel Adams is a wife and the mother of eight children, and a grandmother. She has been writing inspirational romance for over twenty years, and has over thirty published works. Always one to share a message of God's love through her stories, Jewel is a devout Christian Latter-Day Saint who loves the Lord with all her heart and has experienced many blessings and miracles in her life because that love, and she is secure in the knowledge of God's love for her and all men. She is an inspirational and motivational speaker to both youth and adult audiences.

In her spare time, you can find Jewel curled up with a good book and a healthy stash of orange Tic Tacs. She and her family reside in Utah.

Email: jewela40@gmail.com

Websites:

Angelospromise.weebly.com

JewelAdams.com